SNOW SISTER

GW00419725

'The doctor has his personal reasons . . .'
But what can be so mysterious about Dr
Hans Eckhart's private life that no one at
his tiny Swiss clinic will explain his moods
to newly-arrived Sister Fiona Shore?

Books you will enjoy
in our Doctor Nurse series

SNOW SISTER

BY

KATE ASHTON

MILLS & BOON LIMITED
15–16 BROOK'S MEWS
LONDON W1A 1DR

*First published in Great Britain 1985
by Mills & Boon Limited*

© Kate Ashton 1985

*Australian copyright 1985
Philippine copyright 1985*

ISBN 0 263 74984 3

Set in 10 on 11 pt Linotron Times
03–0385–56,116

*Photoset by Rowland Phototypesetting Ltd
Bury St Edmunds, Suffolk
Made and printed in Great Britain by
Richard Clay (The Chaucer Press) Ltd
Bungay, Suffolk*

CHAPTER ONE

FIONA SHORE settled herself in the corner of the tiny railway carriage and tried to absorb the reality of her arrival in Switzerland. The flight from London to Geneva, though far too long for Fiona, had been too short to prepare her for such a different world. Now, on the last leg of her journey, she was still adjusting.

Outside, the little railway station of Lauterbrunnen was humming with activity. Late risers planned their day upon the slopes, clustering around timetables and evidently deciding when they could return to the warmth and comfort of their hotels. For it was eleven by the station clock, Fiona's train was due to leave at five past and all the keenest skiers had departed for the slopes long ago.

Out of the window to her left Fiona could see up the steep slopes of Männlichen mountain to the ridge of conifers behind which nestled the skiing village of Wengen—her destination. Out of the right-hand side window she could watch the railway personnel in their smart uniforms and sunglasses answering queries from travellers, at home in the crystal-clear Alpine morning sunshine.

Fiona could hardly believe that she had really swapped the chilly streets of Elchester for this magical, sparkling world. She kept feeling that she was about to wake up to the dismal awareness that she had overslept and would be late for the beginning of the morning list in General Theatre One at St Helen's Hospital. And she had never once been late for a list since she had taken up her post as theatre sister eighteen months ago . . .

The noisy arrival of a large train at the adjacent platform dispelled Fiona's reverie, and soon swarms of new passengers poured into the little compartment in which she was sitting. The carriage filled up rapidly, leaving only one seat, which happened to be opposite her own, free.

Fiona became gradually aware of the imposing figure who took this seat. A beige raincoat open over his immaculate three piece suit, he took his place without giving her a glance, while a huge St Bernard dog seated itself elegantly at his feet. The dog regarded Fiona steadily, its back turned to its owner.

But Fiona was struck by the man. He appeared strangely out of place among the jostling crowds of skiers, and yet he was utterly at ease on the tiny train. As the engine started up, the stranger stood and pushed the wide window of the carriage down so that he could lean his elbows on it. He stood filling his pipe with tobacco, glancing up from his task every moment or so, casually appreciating the magnificent mountain scenery.

Fiona thought that he looked as though he owned it all. She could not tear her eyes away from the imposing figure. Her side view of him showed a strong profile, as clean in its lines as those of the mountains. His composure matched that of the mountains too. Fiona was fascinated. The stranger closed the window as the train started up the mountainside, and resumed his seat.

The railway track wound upwards through pasture-land dotted with bare beech coppices. Fiona was aware that the man opposite her had lit his pipe and was smoking it, while absent-mindedly stroking his dog. Under the pretext of admiring the dog, Fiona watched the hand that stroked it, noting the carefully manicured nails and the strong sensitivity of the long fingers.

More and more disconcerted by her own fascination with her cool travelling companion, Fiona was pleased when the carriage lights went on and the train entered a tunnel in the mountainside. Now she could study with discretion the reflection of the stranger's profile in his window.

For an instant, Fiona was sure that he was smiling behind the pipe, and then she dismissed the idea as ridiculous. But she did remain certain that he knew how much of her attention he held and was amused by the effect that he was having upon her. She drew her eyes away yet again from the stroking fingers. She thought about how he had stooped at the window and how his stature had been accentuated by the breadth of his shoulders as he had leaned and filled his pipe.

The train emerged from the tunnel into dazzling white sunshine. They were above the snowline now, and glittering fields stretched away on either side of the narrow railway track. The train stopped at a small station and Fiona felt sure that it would start rolling back down the mountain again. She held her breath for an instant, and was certain the man opposite her read her mind and smiled again behind his pipe.

To Fiona's inexpert eyes the skiers who occupied the compartment with her seemed completely at ease in their exotic clothing and surroundings. It did not occur to her that any of them might be complete beginners at the sport. She was awed by the task she had set herself; to learn to ski in just two weeks. But she knew that she desperately needed the complete immersion and concentration that this would require. She desperately needed to forget . . .

Not normally a particularly cautious person, Fiona had resisted the outlay on skiing gear into which she had almost been tempted in the sports shop in Elchester. She had been full of superstition about this holiday; sure that something would stop her from getting here, or that she would never learn to ski if she succumbed to excitement

But now she found herself imagining herself encumbered with more luggage than her one smallish suitcase, burdened with more than her one precious fur coat and simple snow boots. She wondered what it would take for the stranger opposite her to notice her, and she was sure it would need more than the turquoise sweater that so faithfully reflected the colour of her eyes, and the jeans which she was wearing. If she were laden with luggage and in obvious need of help when she got off the train, then perhaps . . .

Fiona blinked guiltily. The eyes of the man were full upon her. She blushed. He was giving her a fair imitation of the appreciative, if condescending look that he had bestowed upon the mountains as he filled his pipe in the valley. Fiona looked out of the window, her pulse racing and her palms becoming moist. This was ridiculous. She could not remember the last time a man had had this effect upon her. Not even Daniel had done so.

Fiona composed herself. The man was looking quietly into the middle distance, puffing calmly on his pipe, stroking his dog. Fiona glanced at her watch. It was almost half-past eleven. The train would be drawing into Wengen very soon.

As the train slowed and before Fiona could see the platform, the tall stranger was on his feet, staring out past her. The station came into view and Fiona caught sight of a group of children running along beside the train. Somebody was about to receive a spectacular welcome, unless this was a routine greeting from small Swiss train-spotters for every arrival, and somehow Fiona doubted that.

The rest of the occupants of Fiona's compartment all seemed to be getting out at Wengen too, and Fiona, eyeing the crush that was forming in the aisle, felt a sudden rush of anxiety. What if she were to get left on the train—if it started up the mountainside again before she had had time to get off? She felt suddenly very alone and vulnerable and had to remind herself severely of her determination to come to Switzerland alone to sort out her bruised feelings.

Blinded by her irrational panic, Fiona reached up to get her suitcase from the wooden luggage rack above her seat, misjudged the weight of it and stepped back inadvertently as she took it in both arms. There was a yelp and then an angry growl behind her and she felt a sudden tight pressure around her ankle. She lifted her foot up off the dog as soon as she had registered what was happening, and simultaneously spun around to confront the dog's owner.

The green eyes that met her stare were, she now clearly saw, flecked with dark grey, and they were lit with anger. Fiona felt her own fury rising in response to the expression that she found in the man's face. She placed her suitcase deliberately down on the seat beside her and waited for him to apologise for his pet. But no apology was forthcoming. Indeed, it seemed that he was waiting for her to speak.

'He bit me!' Fiona exclaimed, outraged.

All around them, skiers pushed one another towards the doors of the tiny train and it seemed to Fiona that she, her adversary and his now contrite dog were arrested in a bubble of time and space of their own.

'You trod on him. What do you expect?' The fine, dark eyebrows were lifted in mild rebuke, but the eyes beneath them were as hard as stone.

Fiona felt the blood rush to her face and she recognised that it was there not in response to her situation, but to the calm features that faced her: the broad, strong mouth, the aristocratic nose and the glacial eyes. She felt humiliated.

Fiona collected her wits, shrugged and, trying to give

the dog a wide berth, attempted to join the throng of disembarking passengers.

'I should not think that he has drawn blood.'

Fiona turned in time to catch the impassive gaze of the stranger as it travelled slowly down towards her jeaned and booted ankle.

'And what if he had?' Fiona demanded furiously, her embarrassment at the renewed contact with the man rising in a tidal wave that threatened to drown her. 'You should have more control over him.'

'I think I should have had full control over *that* situation,' he responded enigmatically, and to his own apparent private amusement.

Fiona did not bother to ponder over this last remark. In fact, she had stepped out on to frozen Swiss soil again before she realised that he had addressed her in perfect, unbroken English.

The little picture-book railway station was hung with mossy baskets which promised summer geraniums, the wooden benches were bright with new paint and the station master presided over his domain with evident satisfaction. But, while he appeared to be enjoying welcoming the noisy skiers who came off the train, it was to one small group of people that he gave his special attention. He had cleared a space within which Fiona was astonished to recognise her recent foe, his features miraculously softened and handsome, scooping up one laughing child while another tugged lovingly at his dark hair.

So this was the reason for the reception committee—*he* was the reason! Fiona looked away. She was uncomfortably aware of a pain that was born in her in that moment. Averting her eyes, she met those of another onlooker. Taller than Fiona's average height, the woman was elegantly dressed in a glossy, dark fur coat.

Her hair shone like a golden halo against the upturned collar; a pair of expensive fur boots were visible beneath the sweeping hemline. But the woman's eyes were her most striking feature. They were chilling, icy aquamarine pools, devoid of warmth even as they witnessed the tender scene before them.

Fiona felt them upon her own face and then, with relief, felt the woman's attention diverted. As if she had taken her fill of the reunion and wanted to end it, the woman turned and strode off up one of the forks of the road that led to the village. Fiona watched, spellbound, as the group of children and father broke up and followed the blonde head. One little girl held each of her father's hands and a small boy, his features childish replicas of those of his father, walked sedately alongside.

Filled with an emotion that she could neither place or name, Fiona watched the family disappearing up the road, while the St Bernard bounded around them, barking his pleasure. She forced herself back into her own reality. Stupid dog, she thought, and rude man! She smiled wryly to herself as the sleek form of the blonde finally disappeared from her view around a curve in the road.

And you can save your frozen glances for some real competition, madam, Fiona thought ferociously, for I am the very last person to be likely to present you with any problems on *that* score! She changed her suitcase into her other hand, squeezed the circulation back into her right one, and began her own ascent into the village.

A few minutes later, Fiona booked herself into an unpretentious *pension*. A sweet-faced landlady led her up to her room, showed her the shower and bath and left her to decide when she would eat. Fiona unpacked. She shook out her precious black silk dress and hung it in the huge wardrobe that stood in her room. She could not imagine what she had been thinking about when she packed the silk dress. It looked completely out of place among all her casual tops and trousers and, after all, she was hardly planning to lead a riotous social life in Wengen.

She undressed slowly, wrapped herself in her towelling bathrobe and went to shower. The hot water worked its usual magic on her. For as long as she could remember, a hot bath or shower had been Fiona's panacea for all ills, and it did not fail her now. By the time she had emerged and dressed in a fresh green jersey and jeans, the tiredness of travelling had disappeared and she was full of new enthusiasm for her holiday. She allowed herself a small, excited bounce on the big pine bed.

It was soft and covered with a feather quilt. A radiator beneath the window warmed the whole room, and the wash-basin and bedside table were spotless. She was going to be happy here for two weeks. She would return to Elchester renewed.

She sat on the edge of the bed and looked out of the window. The mountains stared back agelessly at her and their presence seemed ultimately reassuring. They seemed to tell her that nothing was as bad or important as it now seemed to her; that life was magnificent, nature enduring and the world just waiting for her to explore it.

Fiona knew that she had got into a rut in Elchester, at St Helen's Hospital and even in theatre work. Her best friend, Claire, had even intimated as much when she had last spoken to her on the telephone. Yet now, as she cast her mind back over the last few months, it seemed to Fiona that her real troubles had begun with Claire's departure from Elchester and St Helen's.

It had not seemed strange to Fiona at first that she should miss Claire so much. Claire, whose calm, kind understanding had seen her through so many difficult times, from state registration exams to her last but one love affair. But time had not healed. Since Claire's marriage the flat in Monmouth Gardens had seemed more and more lonely to Fiona and she had not found the heart to advertise for a new flatmate.

Then, within a couple of weeks of the wedding, Fiona's romance with Claire's erstwhile colleague on the renal unit, Tony Fraser, had finally fizzled out as if it had been dependent upon the other couple for its survival. Fiona had not been heart-broken, but she had been saddened by the loss of Tony's company on top of that of Claire and David.

Suddenly, Claire and David Duncan were in Scotland, Tony was gone and Fiona was left holding on to her work as if it was the only solid thing in her life. So that when Daniel Davenport, senior surgical registrar, appeared in General Operating Theatre One, Fiona had been more than susceptible to his many charms.

She had been instantly struck by the physical difference between the new surgeon's golden good looks and the dark, brooding handsomeness of his predecessor, David Duncan. And then she had become aware of other differences between the two surgeons. Where once a serious silence had hung over every operating list, Mr Davenport's sessions were conducted in a mood of cheerfulness and humour. There was even a suggestion of theatrical management in his teaching sessions. Fiona was enchanted, for none of his apparent flippancy detracted from Mr Davenport's consummate skill as a surgeon.

And he had wasted little time in turning his non-professional attention towards his theatre sister. In the weeks that followed his appointment, the new surgeon had paid Fiona exactly the right sort of compliment professionally; exactly the correct amount of personal

attention. He had been discreet but powerfully per-
suasive.

Fiona had been at first flattered, and then swept off
her feet. She had believed this to be the love of her life.
She had discovered a new dimension to work as her
relationship with the surgeon produced an efficiency and
interest which she had never experienced before. And
outside St Helen's she had not been disappointed either.
It seemed as if her instinctive recognition of Daniel
Davenport's skill and experience with women had been
correct.

That the same instincts had warned her of the fatality
of his attraction, and that she had ignored them through
the long summer days of laughter and the long summer
nights of love, had been Fiona's downfall.

She had been far too busy basking in her new happiness to notice how Daniel was slipping away from her.
She had hidden from herself his increasing impatience in
theatre; his uncharacteristic temper tantrums. She had
accepted his flimsy excuses for frequent trips to London
during his precious off-duty time and the dramatic reduction in their meetings that had resulted.

So deep had been her resistance to the idea that she
was losing Daniel that even now she found herself
associating the break-up with a patient rather than with
the new staff nurse. The patient had been a pitifully thin
sixteen-year-old girl whose sweet smile and huge brown
eyes had become the focus of all Fiona's emotional
attention—while the stunning new staff nurse had quite
escaped it.

The patient had been treated two years previously for
her chronic ulcerative colitis, from which distressing
disease she had suffered for six years. A portion of her
bowel had been removed and the remaining healthy
gut re-anastomosed, and she had managed to live a
relatively trouble-free existence since then, provided

that she was careful what she ate. But now she had
been admitted as an emergency with intestinal obstruction, and it was suspected that scar tissue had formed
at the site of her previous operation, blocking off the
bowel.

As soon as the duty surgeon who had seen her in
Casualty had arrived at his provisional diagnosis, the girl
had been rushed up to Female Surgical to be prepared
for emergency surgery. The surgical ward sister had
telephoned Fiona to inform her of the case and Fiona
had freed herself to go down to the ward to see the
patient. Fiona knew how important it was to a patient to
know at least one of the faces behind the masks 'upstairs'.

And, ill though she had been, the girl had shown her
gratitude to Fiona and demonstrated her courage, trying
to whisper her thanks and to smile. Fiona's heart had
gone out to her.

The operation had been far advanced before Daniel
had made his drastic decision. Many of the adhesions
had already been meticulously divided and the lumen of
the bowel cleared before it became clear to him that a
large portion of gut proximal to the obstruction had been
starved of blood for too long and was now necrosed and
nonfunctional.

'Too much here to resect . . .' he had muttered into
his mask. He had broken the unfamiliar silence that had
hung over the tense theatre team for almost two hours.

The significance of Mr Davenport's few words hit
Fiona immediately, and she felt her heart turn over on
behalf of her patient. She knew that Daniel had decided
that he would have to fashion a colostomy; an artificial
opening from the bowel out on to the abdominal wall.
She knew that the girl would have to learn to live with
a very private disfigurement on top of coping with
her chronic illness and all the other problems that

adolescence would throw up at her. Fiona's response was immediate and unconcealed.

'Oh, no. Poor child!' she whispered.

'Sister, how about a little more suction and a little less sentimentality?' Daniel Davenport rasped.

Shocked, Fiona automatically checked the position of the suction head and cautery tip and found that the operation site was being perfectly efficiently cleared of blood and debris and that the surgeon's implied criticism of her assistance had been unfounded.

It was at that exact moment that Fiona first became aware of the patronising gaze of her new staff nurse upon her. The new nurse was standing at her left-hand side, also scrubbed up, and now Fiona knew that she was watching every move that she made. There was an insolence and amusement in her scrutiny that stung Fiona to the quick. It was as if the staff nurse was willing her senior to make a fool of herself.

In the same instant, Fiona decided not to apologise to Mr Davenport. Instead, she watched the surgeon look across and meet the eyes of the new staff nurse and she sensed the smile that passed between them behind their masks.

'I was only expressing my sympathy for the girl,' Fiona said in frozen tones.

'And I was only expressiong my desire for your professional support rather than your non-professional opinion, Sister,' Mr Davenport retorted viciously.

The truth had come to Fiona very late, she now admitted ruefully to herself. The staff nurse had been on her team for almost five weeks when this incident had taken place. Fiona had put it all together by now, but she still had not done so by then; the studied, sarcastic attention that the new nurse had paid during their induction tour of General Theatre One, the barely-veiled contempt in her voice when she had addressed

Fiona as, 'Sister,' and the odd smile that she had been unable to hide when Fiona had formally introduced her to Mr Davenport.

Fiona had played right into their hands. She had been keen to take the staff nurse when a post became suddenly vacant; she had even been flattered that the girl had specifically requested General Theatre One when she had come job-seeking to St Helen's from her London training hospital. Fiona had failed to put two and two together when she had read the headed notepaper that carried the staff nurse's glowing references, even though it originated from the very hospital from which Daniel Davenport had arrived just six months before. What a gullible fool she had been, and how they must have laughed behind her back!

Fiona shook her head and looked deep into the mountains. They seemed to hold her gaze to their cold bosom. She forced herself to relive the final scene between herself and Daniel, as if to do so would be to exorcise it forever from her memory. She faced once again in her mind the terrible, pitying smile that he had given her when at last she had screwed up enough courage to confront him with her suspicions. It had been a smile that told her that she had been the last person at St Helen's Hospital, and possibly in the whole world, to learn the truth about him and Staff Nurse Kelly Morgan. He had not even attempted to deny her wild accusations.

Her humiliation did not allow Fiona to dwell upon how long Daniel Davenport had been having his cake and eating it too. All that mattered to her now was that she was left with both hands full of the burnt ashes of her love affair and that she could see no sign of any rising phoenix.

She had booked this holiday in Switzerland the morning after her break-up with Daniel, as if the chaste

Alpine snow could somehow cleanse her. And now that
she was here she was determined to think positively
about a solitary future. She certainly wanted nothing
more to do with men.

Fiona stood up stiffly and stretched. She really did feel
hungry now. She went over to the wash-basin and
looked at her face in the mirror above it. Her hair had
dried while she day-dreamed and it lay over her shoulders in burnished auburn waterfalls. She gathered it up
and piled it softly on top of her head, carefully pinning
the shining mass in place. Then she looked closely at her
face. It was pretty, she decided; not beautiful, but
distinctly pretty. Her turquoise eyes under their long,
straight lashes smiled back at her.

It could be a positive disadvantage to be pretty. Fiona
had learned this lesson painfully over twenty-six years.
But now she made herself a promise: she would not
settle for relationships based on physical appearances.
That had always been her mistake. And although it was
not the first time that she had promised herself this, she
felt better for the resolve. She put her coat on and
stepped into her boots. She would explore the village
and find something to eat.

The busy village invaded her the moment that she left
the shelter of her little hotel. At the end of the drive that
led up to it Fiona had noticed a little ski-hire shop which
had been almost empty this morning but which was now
buzzing with activity.

Skiers were literally falling over one another in their
enthusiasm to get knitted out and up on to the afternoon
slopes, but in spite of all the apparent chaos, there was
no ill humour on any of the healthy, glowing faces. Their
enthusiasm seemed to be infectious, for Fiona felt her
first flush of anxiety to get into the mountains herself, to
feel the sensation of skiing for herself.

Pausing to peep into the shop, she caught the eye of a fit-looking young man in a sleek red ski suit, whose blond hair, blue eyes and tanned face marked him out from the crowd of paler people. He seemed to be a centre of activity and was currently employed in trying to pull ski boots from the feet of a buxom brunette. The brunette was gasping with exaggerated pain and emitting the occasional expletive in English. Fiona giggled silently.

'I told you they were too tight! That's why I couldn't get up when I fell at the top of the chair-lift,' the girl was grumbling.

'All I hear from you are excuses,' said the blond young man, his accent gently softening all his consonants.

A boot came off suddenly and the young man reeled back into a girl standing behind him; an accident which proved pleasurable, if his expression was anything to go by.

'Honestly, Erich,' wailed his client, 'both my feet are completely numb.'

'Okay. We try one size up,' the young man relented. 'But both ankles must be completely immobile or you will become to harm . . .'

Fiona smiled again at the eccentric use of her own tongue, and at the same time realised that the speaker was looking directly at her. She tried to return his blue, amused look serenely, but it was difficult to look dispassionate in such a comic situation.

'Sheer misery,' the girl in the new ski boot announced, pushing her hair back prettily behind each ear as she did so.

'I know,' winked her helper, 'but think of the pictures you will take home to show your friends.'

'Oh, yes! Me sitting in the snow at the top of a chair-lift, unable to get up. I felt like a stranded sheep.'

If the girl needed confirmation of her fleeting appearance in this unflattering role she needed at that moment only to glance at her companion's face.

'Pig!' she said plaintively.

'Wolf!' he corrected, with a mock growl and a charming grin.

The pair made for the door of the little shop, she with an exaggeratedly hobbling step, leaning a little too heavily on his arm. He made sure that Fiona was in their path.

'Are you also English?'

Fiona's surprise at being directly addressed must have shown in her face, for the young man laughed aloud, displaying his set of perfect white teeth.

'I am so sorry,' he said merrily. 'I should have known better than to speak to an English girl before we have been introduced.'

The girl on his arm threw Fiona an irritated glance.

'I am Erich,' the young man offered. 'I teach skiing here in Wengen. Are you here to ski?'

'Er, yes. That is, I think so,' Fiona stammered, feeling foolish at her own lack of self-confidence. She shook hands with the ski instructor, unable any longer to ignore his extended arm.

'Fiona,' she said, slightly unwillingly. 'Fiona Shore.'

'Good,' said Erich with an air of finality. 'I will see you again soon, Fiona.'

Fiona recoiled from the intimacy in his use of her first name. But she returned his smile. Why was it that English men never looked like this, she wondered? The silken blond hair, the shining teeth and the blueness of Erich's eyes seemed to have made an indelible impression upon her. But it was the sun-tan that produced the devastating effect, she decided. And looks were only skin deep.

Still, she watched Erich leave the shop, his slim form a pliant support for the rather substantial young lady who leaned possessively towards him, and Fiona got the district impression that both characters were playing their parts for her benefit.

CHAPTER TWO

FIONA had found a charming little restaurant in which to eat, had explored the village for another couple of hours and then returned to the hotel for the rest of her first evening in Wengen. Now, after nine hours of deep sleep, she got up early, showered, dressed warmly and went downstairs to breakfast. She discovered the fresh bread and butter and home-made jam as if they were the first she had ever tasted, and drank two cups of coffee that made her wonder how the British dared to call their beverage by the same name.

At last she stepped outside into the sparkling Alpine morning, and the fresh air almost took her breath away. She had decided to take a path that had tempted her when, over her supper the night before, she had searched her map for walks. She turned right outside the little ski shop and started up the hill out of the village, along a summer farm track which wound past the outlying chalets.

The village behind her, Fiona followed the track upwards through pastureland which was now a perfect snowscape of softly curving shadow. She entered a fir forest, finding that she had to stop every now and then to recover her breath.

Each time she stopped, she looked around her in amazement at a hidden world of icicles, frosted bark and heavenly pine-scented sunshine. Here and there she glimpsed the tracks left by some tiny secretive creature, and she was enchanted by the thought of all this life going on, far from the world of the skiing tourists.

At last she caught sight of the coppice that harboured

her goal: a vantage point signposted Leiterhorn, from which she should be able to see all the way down into the valley. She longed to see Lauterbrunnen from up here, and the little village of Gündlischwand, beside which fled the glacial stream of milky turquoise water which she had glimpsed from the train. If the sky remained clear it would be well worth the climb.

As the last lap of her climb began, Fiona found her thoughts returning to St Helen's Hospital, and she was glad to have them banished by the strange sound of high voices in the still, cold air. They sounded far away, like fairy voices, and Fiona stopped in her tracks, trying with all her senses to locate them.

But scan the mountain though she might, she could find no sign of the origin of the voices, and no sooner had she stopped moving than the elusive sounds disappeared and she was left doubting whether she had heard them at all. Around her, the deep white silence of the mountains echoed her own quietness.

She continued to climb slowly, accepting the strain that the unaccustomed altitude was putting upon her body and letting that, rather than her mind, dictate her pace. She was in no hurry, after all. Entering another thicket of woodland, Fiona found herself ascending steps fashioned out of the roots of the trees that surrounded her path, and ahead she could just make out a small clearing. Suddenly, she heard again the sound of voices, much closer this time, and then she could see the colours of clothing.

In another minute Fiona emerged into the clearing. The three children had their backs to her, leaning side by side at the safety railing that bounded the vantage point, kicking little flurries of snow out from beneath it into space. A little distance away, leaning her back against a pine tree and looking in the vague direction of the children, Fiona saw the blonde woman.

Fiona regretted that she had come too close to the group to turn back unseen – for that had been her first instinct upon recognising them. But now the children turned round, with that animal awareness that children have of another's presence, and their faces confirmed them as those of the rapturous platform welcome of yesterday.

The two rosy-cheeked girls greeted Fiona's arrival on the ridge with shy smiles, but their brother, his face so clearly reminiscent of his father's, offered Fiona a welcome in his own language.

Fiona felt her heart turn over with an unwelcome shock.

'Hello,' she nervously returned. Why did the child have this effect upon her? She wished that he had not spoken to her. She wanted to run, to escape. It was ridiculous.

'You are English?' the boy politely enquired.

'Yes,' Fiona asserted, 'I am here on holiday.'

She had felt compelled to answer, to offer extra information in response to this frank, flecked gaze.

'I saw you yesterday,' he told her.

'Yes,' Fiona said quickly. 'How good your English is.'

She needed to change the subject, and yet she felt as though his dignified demeanour demanded that she treat him as an adult. He is exactly like his father, Fiona thought, and, as if it needed strengthening, her impression was underlined by the appearance upon the boy's face of a mysterious smile. Fiona's mind flashed back to the enigmatic smile that had accompanied her train companion's last remark to her.

'That is nice of you,' said the boy unaffectedly. 'We all get English lessons from . . .'

His sentence was interrupted by a furious glance from the blonde woman. Galvanised by her silent message, the boy signalled to his sisters and all three made off out

of the clearing after the retreating figure of the woman.
Fiona was left alone.

But she had caught for the second time in as many
days the full impact of that lovely, cold face; the sym-
metry of those features and the clarity of the porcelain
complexion. She knew that the woman had been
angered by the boy talking to her. Fiona felt her stomach
knotting as she unconsciously compared her own ped-
estrian prettiness to that stunning beauty. She admitted
to herself wistfully how physically unforgettable the
father had been too. They certainly made a striking
couple; a perfect family.

Fiona turned and looked blindly out from her vantage
point into the snow-filled sky. It was no good thinking
about them – *him*. She would get back to the village and
get herself organised for skiing tomorrow. After all,
that was what she was here for, not to complicate her
emotional life even further.

As if to reinforce her conviction, some divine force
chose that moment to part the clouds and show her the soft
valley far below. She saw the villages with their toy-town
railway stations and the plunging stream that ran beside
the track. Opposite, she glimpsed the snowy heights of
Schynige Platte before the clouds once more closed off
her view. And suddenly the loneliness of the mountains
filled her, and Fiona longed to be among people in the
village again.

She took a logger's track back down towards Wengen.
Her map had shown her that this was a short cut,
following the forest in a broad swathe that swept down
the mountainside in great curves. The snow crunching
beneath her feet, Fiona soon came upon evidence of
other people having recently passed down this way, and
it was not long before she recognised the three sets of
small footprints accompanied by a larger set.

Fiona cursed softly under her breath and slowed her

pace. In spite of her anxiety to get back to the village, she could not bear the thought of running into the family again. Just the thought of the children—especially of the boy—was enough to disturb her composure. She looked at her map and discovered that, once having chosen this path down, she had no option but to continue to follow it.

On either side of the track tall fir trees swayed in the glittering air. Fiona tried to concentrate on the beauty of her surroundings rather than upon the people whose descent she followed so closely. It was three-quarters of an hour before she came across a signpost which told her that Wengen was only another kilometre away, and her step quickened involuntarily at the thought of the hot chocolate that she had promised herself. It seemed an age since she had finished her breakfast.

At the edge of the ridge that she had climbed, Fiona emerged from the forest and saw the village spread out below her. It was a welcome sight. The rough track turned into a snow-covered tarmac road here, and the first of the outlying houses of the village lay a few yards ahead.

Glancing to her left, Fiona saw a steep terrace of steps that had been cut into the mountainside beside the forest's edge. Her gaze was drawn upwards towards the magnificent house that nestled there, while she became aware that the footprints that she had been following had stopped and gone off the road at this point. Sure enough, the snow on the narrow terrace of steps had been freshly disturbed.

Fiona stopped dead and held her breath for a long moment. Then she let it out in a low whistle of astonishment. The house at which she stared had the same deep eaves of its sister chalets in the village, but its windows were much larger than any she had seen up until now. Across the front of the house at first-floor level was a broad wooden balcony from which the view of the mountains would be, Fiona knew, magnificent.

Above the balcony, a row of shuttered windows hid the bedrooms. But it was the ground floor that really held her attention. The wooden slatted frontage of the house had been ornately painted with stylised flower designs in green, red, gold and gentian blue at this level and, sheltered by the overhanging balcony, wide french windows opened off an enormous uncurtained room.

Behind the french windows, Fiona looked into the pine interior of this magnificent room, the supporting beams of which ran its whole length. Upon the floor was a thick white carpet, and sparse pine and white-upholstered furniture completed the impression of muted opulence. From where she stood in the road, Fiona could just see a large circular table at the far end of the room, and make out the pastel shades of the land-scape paintings which dominated the dining area.

Two Siamese cats watched her from behind the french windows, blinked, stretched and then moved away across the white carpet, evidently bored by her. Fiona wondered for how long they had been silently scrutinising her, returning her stare. They unsettled her— reminded her of something, or someone . . .

Fiona's reverie was interrupted by a sudden aware-ness of somebody walking into the room into which she was staring. She felt a prick of embarrassment at her own rudeness, but it was too late now to turn away and pretend to have been simply passing by.

The recognition was mutual. The cold eyes of the blonde had rested unmistakably upon Fiona and she had felt their disdain and suspicion. Cold, calculating cat's eyes. That was what she had been reminded of by the Siamese.

Her feet numb from standing still for so long on the

frozen road, Fiona gathered her coat more closely around her and made for the village. All the way there she fought the shame of her intrusive stare and its discovery. She must avoid that part of the village from now on, that was painfully obvious. She never wanted to encounter that woman again.

Over a bowl of warming goulash soup, Fiona permitted herself one last day-dream about what it would be like to eat lunch at that circular table, surrounded by beautiful paintings. Looking out of the restaurant window, she allowed herself to dream just for a moment about what it would be like to walk bare-footed across that white carpet one morning, to throw open the french windows upon a sun-drenched mountain view.

Then she forced herself to think about her own life: the flat in Monmouth Gardens, St Helen's, the operating theatre, and to accept that she lived in a different world. It was no good dreaming about these other lives; she had to live her own. Wealth did not necessarily mean happiness, she told herself, a fact that she sometimes found hard to believe when her meagre pay packet arrived at the end of each month.

Fiona swallowed the rest of her soup, although her hunger had fled. She knew that the next step in this train of thought would involve Daniel. The thought of Daniel—happy, smiling that special smile which she had come to hope was for her alone—was more than she could bear. She paid her bill and walked briskly out and down the street towards the ski-hire shop near her *pension*. It was clear that she could not afford to have an empty mind at the moment. She pushed the door of the shop open.

Inside there was the same atmosphere that she had sensed on her first day here, but the shop was not crowded now. She was amazed, now that she was properly inside, at the sheer quantity of stuff that was crammed into it. She did not have a clue where to begin in equipping herself for this sport.

'Can I help you?'

A tall, pleasant-looking girl approached her.

'Thank you,' Fiona responded gratefully. 'How did you know I was English?'

'I heard Erich talking to you yesterday,' the girl said.

'Well, I suppose I need everything,' smiled Fiona, shrugging helplessly.

'Fine. Let's begin with boots,' the girl said. Fiona decided that she would enjoy this session. It was nice to talk to somebody.

'Thank goodness for that,' she exclaimed, as the assistant pronounced the seventh pair of ski boots perfect. They gripped her ankles like a vice. Fiona gritted her teeth and smiled.

'Which party are you with?' the shop girl asked, obviously trying to distract Fiona from the business of removal of the boots.

'Er, none,' said Fiona, wincing.

'But you cannot possibly ski alone!'

Fiona hardly liked to admit that she had not given this a thought. The practicalities, like the reality of the Alps, had seemed a million miles away until this moment. She had had some hazy idea that she would find a school or an instructor, or whatever.

'I wanted to come alone, actually,' Fiona began. She suddenly felt a desire to confide in the quiet girl at her feet, as if she would understand.

'Sometimes it is a good plan to be alone,' the girl agreed, before Fiona had said any more, and Fiona sensed her sympathy.

A little later, she stood in front of the full-length mirror at the back of the shop, trying hard to recognise herself. She was wearing a red quilted ski suit comprising dungaree-style trousers and a short fitted jacket, which looked and felt good over her own white polo-neck sweater. She was surprised at how slim and fit she looked—and how like all the glamorous skiers whose appearance she had admired since arriving in Wengen. But this was just the beginning.

'You look super,' the assistant told her enthusiastically. 'You really must take that suit.'

'Yes. You really must.'

Fiona turned in time to catch the delighted smile which accompanied Erich's frank admiration of her appearance. He was standing close by, hands on his slim hips, head on one side.

Fiona tried hard to remain cool under his gaze.

'Thank you. Yes, I'll take it for the fortnight, then,' Fiona told the girl, ignoring Erich.

'And how do you learn to ski?' he asked her back.

'I haven't decided about that yet,' Fiona carefully replied.

She glanced at the shop assistant who was leaning against the mirror watching the scene as if she had seen it many, many times before. Perhaps she's in love with him, thought Fiona fleetingly. Poor girl!

'I'm cheap, and I'm free tomorrow morning,' Erich invited. 'You are a complete beginner?'

'Yes,' Fiona admitted, 'but I'm not sure whether I want to take private lessons or join a school.' This was the truth. She did not like the assumption behind Erich's invitation.

'Please yourself. The offer's there,' he said, winking at her.

He breezed out of the shop, blowing a kiss in the general direction of the shop assistant, which she acknowledged with a resigned shrug of her shoulders.

'Not very subtle,' she said, reading Fiona's mind, 'but he is a very good instructor, possibly the best in Wengen, if you can take the pace.'

She's nice, thought Fiona, more convinced than ever that the girl would understand her reasons for coming to Wengen on her own.

'He moves fast, eh?' Fiona asked lightly. 'Well, we all know his type.'

The assistant smiled ruefully.

'Anyway, I'd take him up on his offer if I were you,' she said. 'He is good, and he doesn't ask just anybody.'

'Here's to ulterior motivation,' smiled Fiona, lifting her coffee-cup in a mock toast. The assistant joined her in it.

Erich chose that moment to reappear and inform Fiona that he could not wait to hear her decision.

'I'll be glad to have a lesson tomorrow morning,' she told him with cool courtesy. 'Thank you.'

'Fine. Ten o'clock all right?' he asked.

'Thank you. Yes. Fine.'

'And what about tonight?'

Fiona could not contain her gasp of surprise, in spite of the recent warning. She looked quickly at the assistant, who shrugged again and gave her the ghost of a smile.

'Tonight I'm going to wash my hair,' Fiona said.

From the assistant's face it was plain that the excuse was an international one.

'Ah. That is a shame,' said Erich uncertainly. He was clearly thrown by Fiona's evident immunity to his charm. 'Ten o'clock tomorrow then, here.'

Fiona nodded and looked away.

She felt greatly pleased with herself. She was obviously not so susceptible as she had feared that she might be, and actually capable of remaining impervious to a man as handsome as the ski instructor. There was hope for her yet! She was going to survive. She was even going to be happy alone. And tomorrow . . . tomorrow she would begin to learn to ski.

Erich gave his pupil the benefit of his dazzling smile.

'Ready?'

Fiona did not feel ready. She was extremely nervous. The rested feeling with which she had awoken this morning, the feeling that St Helen's and even Daniel belonged on another planet, had disappeared. Suddenly, she devoutly wished herself back in Elchester. Skiing looked like an assault course designed with her annihilation specifically in mind.

Erich, however, looked super-confident this morning. Dressed in a black ski suit which hugged his lean frame and accentuated his sleek figure, he looked blonder than ever and his sun-tan was even more flattering.

Fiona glanced unhappily at her instructor. If Erich had been an ugly brute it would be easier to contemplate the day ahead. But the idea of being watched and of making a fool of herself in front of this suave stranger definitely did not appeal to her. The fact that she knew that she looked the part, resplendent in her new red ski suit, did little to comfort her.

'You look good to eat,' Erich informed her.

'Good enough to eat,' Fiona corrected him absentmindedly. It took all her powers of concentration simply to walk in her ski boots.

'And how do you feel?' Erich asked.

But he was silenced by a look from his new pupil.

After that, Erich transformed himself into the professional for which he was obviously known and respected. He was a patient, kind and responsible teacher, and Fiona quickly gained confidence. She was amazed and delighted to find that she had mastered the nursery slopes by the time lunch beckoned them to the warmth of a nearby café.

It was true that she had fallen quite a lot at first, but Erich had treated this as a matter of course, so that Fiona herself was philosophical by the end of the morning.

Erich had helped her to her feet with reassuring words and in fact her only humiliation had come at the hands of the host of tiny skiers who had borne down upon her with frightening speed and suddenness just as she was getting up from her last fall.

They were obviously using the nursery slopes simply as a short cut down into the village from higher slopes, and were weaving and whooping their way down the *piste*, scattering and terrifying any bemused beginner who happened to be in their path.

Fiona's fury at being almost knocked into the snow again by mere children was matched only by her admiration of their skill and technique. She gazed after the miniature skiers open-mouthed, and it was not until they had come to a kaleidoscopic standstill that she was able to recognise the three children from the big house. Immaculately kitted out in blue, yellow and red ski suits, their beauty stood out among the crowd. Fiona quickly averted her eyes, hoping that they had not seen her too.

She turned to Erich, trying to hide her confusion.

'Well, if they can do it, I'm damn sure that I can too,' she murmured.

But Erich had recognised only the familiar beginner's admiration for his countrymen's early skill on skis.

'They learn to ski before they can walk,' he told her pleasantly.

Fiona nodded. But she was thinking of something else. It seemed that a mere glimpse of those three small faces could plunge her back into speculation about her erstwhile train companion and, rationalise though she might, she could not come to terms with the impact that he had made upon her.

Fiona collected her skis from outside the café. She was alone, Erich having been called to a conversation with a

ski instructor colleague. He had promised to meet her at
the station as soon as he was free.

A whole blissful afternoon of practice stretched ahead.
Already graduated from the busy nursery slopes, Fiona
and Erich were heading for the slightly more difficult
ones higher up the mountain, and Fiona was thrilled by
the progress that this implied. She walked through the
village towards the station dreamily, her skis over her
shoulder. She was beginning to feel like a real skier at
last.

She looked lazily at the shop windows as she walked,
taking in the furs, the lovely soft Italian leather goods
and the expensive evening dresses. She thought wistfully of her precious black silk dress hanging in the
wardrobe in her hotel room. In Elchester it had always
looked so special; here she thought it dull and drab.
Fiona chided herself for the whisper of discontent
that had intruded on her afternoon. It was just too easy
to imagine the bliss of living here; too easy and too
disturbing.

Suddenly, she became aware of an oddly familiar
smell of tobacco. She stopped and looked into a small
shop, the window of which was crammed full of intri-
cately-carved pipes. Each pipe bowl represented a
tiny, unique face, and each face seemed to return her
fascinated gaze.

The interior of the shop was dark behind the window,
but Fiona could just make out the form of a customer
inside. As her eyes got used to their new focus, her
recognition of that beige tailored raincoat, those broad
shoulders and an unmistakable physique grew until
there was no doubt about their owner.

She was about to set briskly off down the road when he
emerged from the shop. Fiona, her heart banging
against her ribcage, pretended to scrutinise the pipes in
the window while the man stooped to avoid the low lintel

of the doorway and then paused calmly outside the shop to light his pipe.

The familiar dog had followed him enthusiastically out into the sunlit street. Fiona took a deep breath and held it for a long moment as if to make herself invisible. But the dog, seeing her, stopped dead in its tracks. Fiona was certain that the dog could not have remembered her from the train. It must simply be wary of all strangers.

There was no way in which Fiona could avoid for any longer the silent regard of the dog's owner, whom she supposed was having difficulty in recalling her. She met the flecked eyes without flinching, and found mild amusement in them.

'It's all right, Carl. Calm down, old chap,' he said, looking down at the dog.

Fiona was furious. He was speaking exaggerated English to the animal, purely for her benefit; to make her feel even more uncomfortable than she obviously was already. She struggled to find an apt reply, or some way of showing her annoyance, but it was too late.

The man patted his pet's head as if to placate him, and then set off down the street as if nothing had happened and Fiona did not exist.

Walking mechanically towards the station again, Fiona wondered why she should feel so hurt that he had treated her with such amused indifference. After all, he was an almost total stranger, and a rather rude and superior one too. She fought the disappointment that his obvious struggle to remember her had caused. For after all, their encounter on the train had been brief and of no significance in comparison with the reunion which had awaited him upon the platform.

But there were other things about the man that Fiona pondered over. He dressed in a style more suitable for the smart streets of Geneva than for those of a skiing village. He seemed somehow removed from the tourist bustle of the village. What could he do for a living? Fiona's mind ran over possibilities. He could be a bank manager, a lawyer . . . a consultant surgeon? She smiled wryly to herself. Trust me, she thought!

'Hey, where do you think you're going?'

Fiona felt a firm arm on her shoulder and looked round into Erich's blue eyes.

'You have taken a long path to the station. I saw you and followed, luckily. You have been dreaming. Perhaps of me?' He lifted his eyebrows hopefully.

Whatever admirable qualities Erich possessed, modesty did not feature among them.

'Actually, no, Erich,' Fiona told him frostily. But she felt sorry for him the moment that her words were out. He did not mean to be so crass and overbearing, and how was he to know how vulnerable she had been feeling at that moment?

A little while later, as the train climbed up towards the intermediate *pistes*, Fiona had a chance to look carefully at the handsome face of her instructor. It belonged to a young man who was used to having a good time and not worrying about it. Maybe, she reflected, she was being foolish in refusing to join in the *après-ski* fun with all the others. It would not have been in keeping with her old nature to hold back like this, and it was not as if anybody was seriously trying to seduce her. The past year had apparently banished her light heart forever.

She thought briefly and bitterly about Tony's sulks and Daniel's charm and duplicity. She had learned her lesson, but did that mean that she had to sentence herself to a fun-free existence? Surely not.

So, when Erich invited her out to dinner that evening, Fiona had already decided to accept his offer. The sun had fallen behind the far mountains and the snow had turned the silver blue that heralded night. Fiona took off her skis and straightened her back to find Erich standing very close.

'First mulled wine,' he said, 'and then dinner. To celebrate your very good progress.'

'And your very good instruction,' she returned.

The café to which Erich took her to sample her very first mulled wine was full of fresh-faced skiers who looked as exhilarated as Fiona felt. She took off her woolly hat and shook her burnished hair free.

'I feel great!' she said happily.

'You look great,' Erich echoed.

The *Glühwein* was mysterious, steaming, rich and aromatic. Fiona inhaled the heady perfume of lemons, cloves and cinnamon and thought that she had never smelled anything quite so delicious in her life. It was an unforgettable experience to let the hot liquor slip down her throat, leaving a warm and scented path behind it.

The warm wine, the compliment from her ski instructor and the real pleasure that she was beginning to discover on this solitary holiday all seemed magically to combine to produce a sense of elation inside Fiona. She looked forward to the evening ahead.

Freshly showered and dressed in the pink cord trousers that she had not thought she would ever dare to wear when she'd bought them, Fiona searched her pile of sweaters for the pink angora one. Beneath the shelf of jumpers hung the silk dress of which she had felt briefly ashamed this afternoon. Now it gave her a wistful sensation in the pit of her stomach. She loved that dress. The last time that she had worn it, she had gone with her newly widowed father to a cocktail party at his firm. He had been very proud of her—and she of his courage and quiet strength.

Men of her own age bored Fiona. It was a secret which she kept to herself, always longing for it to be disproved.

But it never was. Or, at least, her only two serious affairs had failed to disprove it to her. Men of her own age had been incapable of making her feel cherished for herself. They had demanded payment in kind for every display of affection, every gesture. She had hoped that things would be different with Daniel, not least because they had worked so well together, but she had been deeply disappointed.

She pulled her soft angora sweater over her head and arranged her hair. She tried to put aside such thoughts, and had managed to do so by the time she met Erich. He looked excitingly different tonight, in jeans and an open-necked shirt, and Fiona was again surprised at his clean good looks.

A glass of wine later, she felt even more relaxed. Erich was being charming, explaining the secret art of fondue-making while they waited for their own meal to arrive, and being generally attentive and amusing. Only once or twice did Fiona find her attention wandering.

Once, she looked up from the red and white checked table-cloth and wondered what it must be like to eat at one of the smart hotels here in Wengen. Once, she scanned the handsome face across the table from her and saw emptiness behind the smile, behind the blue eyes, and her thoughts drifted to other eyes . . . calm, amused expressive eyes, amazingly flecked with dark grey . . .

Outside the restaurant, Erich took Fiona's arm and she submitted to his familiar touch because of the security it afforded her in the icy streets of the village as much as on the ski slopes.

'Cross here,' he commanded at one point, and Fiona almost slipped and fell at the sudden change in direction. She felt Erich's hold on her tighten.

'Where are we going?' Fiona enquired. It had been a long day. She longed for bed, but it seemed churlish to abandon Erich so soon after he had bought her dinner

'Dancing.'

Fiona's heart sank.

It was hot inside the night-club. They had gone through two sets of doors and found a small table near a circular dance floor. A soft rosy light fell upon the circle where one or two couples were moving slowly, closely held in one another's arms. The music was soft and low.

'It gets, how you say it, a bit more live later on,' Erich said, seeing her watching the dancers.

'Oh, I think it's live enough for me as it is,' Fiona laughed. 'I feel half-dead! It must be all the wine and food you gave me.'

'You will have another glass of wine?'

'Oh, no, thank you Erich. I'll never be able to ski tomorrow at this rate,' Fiona told him.

'You must live for tonight.'

Erich ordered more wine for himself and mineral water for Fiona. The water was welcome, cool and refreshing in the thick atmosphere of the club.

'Will you dance?' Erich asked in a moment.

Fiona shook her head. The music had altered dramatically in mood and was now throbbing West Indian raggae, which fell around them in waves and made normal speech impossible.

'No?' Erich insisted.

Fiona shook her head again, even more vehemently, but then Erich was on his feet in front of her, and Fiona was pulled to hers. Before she could resist, he had whisked her towards the dance floor and she had found herself in the middle of the throng of dancers. The rhythm of the music was forcing a response from her unwilling limbs.

Erich moved, a mesmerising figure in the flickering strobe lights, and Fiona could do nothing but move too. She began to forget herself completely, responding naturally to the music until at last the drums faded and the song came to an end.

Breathless, her face flushed under the lights, Fiona found her hand grasped by Erich as the lights softened. She hoped that he would lead her from the circle, but instead he held her firmly beside him. A low melody began which led into the melancholoy Bob Marley song 'No Woman no Cry'. For some reason, Fiona felt like doing just that.

Erich was close to her and as the small dance floor filled up again, she was forced into his arms. She felt the hair of his chest beneath her cheek and inhaled the dark, masculine smell of his skin, damp after the exertion of the last dance. Fiona moved so that her head was resting on Erich's shoulder against the clean cotton of his shirt. The feel of his naked skin on her face had been disturbing. She took a deep breath and felt Erich's instant response. His supple body demanded submission to his embrace, and her body had to fight to deny it.

Fiona concentrated on the end of the dance and her chance to excuse herself and escape. She knew it had been a mistake to come here with Erich, and now she was paying for her own lack of conviction. Suddenly, she felt her head turned forcibly, and his mouth was hard upon her unwilling lips. She fought for breath and somehow freed both hands and pushed against his hard chest. He let her go and she reeled backwards into a group of people standing at the edge of the dance floor.

'Don't do that again, Erich! Ever,' she gasped, recovering her balance.

And then she fled. She pushed her way out through the drinkers and dancers towards the first set of doors. She grabbed her coat from the crowded rack in the cloakroom and pulled it across her shoulders as she made for the exit. Once outside the night-club she stopped and, her heart racing, took a deep breath of night air. The star-filled sky above her seemed to look down protectively upon her.

She was deciding where exactly in the village she was and which road she should take back to her hotel when a Mercedes drew up at the kerb beside her. Fiona hardly noticed it, so busy was she trying to get her bearings in case Erich should find her out here, and so it was with a shock that she registered a low, masculine voice. The driver of the car was obviously addressing her, for there was nobody else anywhere near.

'May I offer you assistance? You look somewhat, er, distressed.'

Fiona was stunned to hear that cultivated accent again. She stooped and looked into the moonlit face of the car-driver, and met the level gaze from his extraordinary eyes. They did not leave her face for a moment.

Fiona gulped back her exclamation of surprise and composed herself as best she could.

'Thank you so much, but no. I'm fine . . .' she smiled. But she heard her own words with astonishment. What was she saying?

'Indeed?' The voice was deep, full of genuine concern.

'You are very kind,' Fiona faltered.

'May I offer you a lift somewhere? To your hotel, perhaps?'

Fiona felt numb with emotion; dumb with confusion.

'Fiona!' Erich's strident voice broke in upon her like a thunder-clap. The price for her indecision! The ski instructor caught her roughly by both shoulders and spun her round to face him.

'Erich!' Fiona exclaimed, her bitter anger and anguish at the interruption rising up and filling her. She had a blindingly clear vision of how all this would look to the silent, watching car-driver. She tore her eyes away from Erich and looked towards the Mercedes. A glimpse told

her that her fears were realised. He had started the
engine. He thought that she was pleased to see Erich.

She heard a muted, polite, 'Goodnight,' before the
car purred away.

Fiona felt like running after it, or screaming, or hitting
Erich—or all three. The only opportunity which would
probably ever present itself for her to turn her dreams of
a certain man into some sort of reality had just passed
her by. She turned her attention to Erich.

'What do you want?' she demanded icily.

'To find you. I did not know where you had gone—I
did not think you . . .'

'That is just the trouble, Erich. You did not think.
You never think at all.'

She was surprised by the venom in her own voice, but
it helped to let out some of the bitterness that had welled
up inside her. Erich's hands had dropped woodenly to
his sides and he was looking hopelessly at her.

'I know that Swiss girls feel . . . as you do. But foreign
girls. Well, you know?'

'I do *not* know,' Fiona exclaimed furiously. 'I have
done nothing to encourage your advances, Erich. I have
paid you for skiing lessons and that is all. You do not
seem to understand where friendship begins and ends.'
She stopped and caught her breath.

'I think I understand now, Fiona,' Erich said. 'I shall
walk with you to your hotel so that you will know that I
am sorry.'

Fiona avoided looking at her silent companion as they
walked through the empty village streets to her hotel.
And she kept a clear metre of pavement between them.
Her inner self still seethed with rage against him for his
inopportune arrival on the scene a short time ago, and
against herself for her stupid indecision.

Thoughts of what might have been preoccupied and
tortured her all the way home, and it was not until she

was fumbling for her key outside the darkened hotel that she became really aware of the miserable Erich.

'I'm sorry,' she said, wearily. 'I didn't mean to be so savage with you, Erich, but you shouldn't have pounced on me like that . . .'

'You will trust me from now on?' Erich asked. 'You will have a lesson tomorrow?'

Fiona smiled at his tone of voice, and nodded her assent.

It was almost three o'clock in the morning before she slipped under the duvet at last. But she could not sleep. The events of the evening paraded themselves before her tired eyes again and again. She knew that she had been unfair to Erich and that her earlier behaviour could easily have led him to think that his romantic overtures would not be rejected. And yet she hated him for that brutal kiss. She knew that the driver of the Mercedes, whom fate had placed again accidentally in her path, had totally misread Erich's presence outside the night-club.

It was hopeless. Fiona despaired of herself. She must forget about the man. She knew that he was married, that he was rich and that he lived a life of which she could never be a part. She was torturing herself to no good purpose with her imaginings.

Yet she could not stop herself from wondering what he had been doing out in the streets of Wengen so late, alone. She found herself wishing that he might have sensed the truth of her situation with Erich. And she knew that she longed to see him again, in spite of everything.

The snowy Alpine night was giving way to silver-grey morning by the time Fiona fell asleep, relinquishing at last her mental hold on that face, knowing that she was too tired even to dream about it.

CHAPTER THREE

'You ARE not feeling too tired, I hope?'

Erich's question was genuinely concerned. Fiona, noting the small frown that furrowed the brow of her ski instructor, was grateful to him for not bearing malice over last night's episode. She could not have borne spending this glorious day with a sulky companion.

She reassured him. In fact she had slept well, however briefly, and she felt refreshed. The two set off for the station, easy in one another's company, and Fiona felt satisfied that she had managed to place their relationship back on neutral ground. In fact, she felt as if she could afford some spiritual generosity.

'I'd like to buy you supper tonight, Erich,' she said, to his obvious surprise, 'so that we're quits and you don't get any more funny ideas about me.'

She gave him a sidelong glance and caught the fleeting smile that passed across his features before he replied.

'Funny ideas? I do not see what you can mean,' he said, eyebrows innocently raised.

'Oh, no?'

Erich gave her the benefit of his devastating smile.

The sun shone brilliantly upon the snow fields, illuminating the toy-like pylons, cabins and cables which carried the colourful skiers up and down the mountains. The train carrying Erich and Fiona climbed laboriously up from Wengen to Kleine Scheidegg.

Fiona knew that she could not sit in the mountain train without having disturbing thoughts about her first encounter with the tall stranger, but this morning that

44

memory was overshadowed by another, more recent one.

It sat stubbornly in the centre of her mind, threatening her enjoyment of the day ahead. The more she recognised the pointlessness of brooding upon it, the more she re-lived the encounter.

She had told herself a hundred times this morning that her obsession with a married man who thought her merely a silly tourist was madness. Yet the obsession remained. She was glad when the train stopped at their station and Erich gestured her to follow him out. It was just as well, she told herself as she did so, that he had interrupted her meeting with the driver of the Mercedes.

Fiona applied herself with grim determination to her skiing. She managed to master the art of getting on and off the chair-lift without either falling or leaving her skis tangled up in the apparatus. She harboured a secret thrill at each advance that increased her independence and brought the time nearer when she would be able to sample the delights of skiing alone.

In the afternoon she managed to convert her clumsy 'snowplough' stop into an altogether more elegant and dignified 'stem-christiana' turn, and she was truly exultant. Erich's own pleasure in Fiona's progress was evident from his quiet nods of approval and the speed with which he took her on from one step to the next.

Just once or twice during the morning, Fiona glanced at her handsome tutor and wondered why it was that she had so minded being kissed by him last night. Had she over-reacted to his advances? But she pushed the distracting thoughts away, unable to cope with them as well as with the vagaries of the ski slopes. Erich, as if he sensed the brief lapses in her resistance to him, was particularly charming all day.

'I suppose it's a silly question to ask you to dance this

evening?' he enquired as they sipped coffee after the unpretentious meal that Fiona had bought them that early evening.

'Very silly,' Fiona confirmed gently. 'I think I'll stick to skiing and eating the odd, well-lit meal with you,' she teased, adding a, 'Thank you anyway,' to soften her message.

'You are a hard girl, Fiona,' Erich told her with a shake of his head.

'I know. I know,' Fiona replied. 'That is what people always say about us nurses. When you are not calling us angels, that is.'

Erich was clearly taken completely by surprise.

'A nurse? But I should have known. Nurses are a special sort of people,' he breathed.

Fiona smiled. It was astonishing the effect that this piece of information had on many people. She had never quite been able to get over the high regard in which members of her profession were held by the lay public, especially as she knew just how fallible she herself could be.

She met the new regard and respect in Erich's expression.

'Oh, I don't know that we are as special as all that,' she said lightly. 'Of course, the nurses you've met may be, for all I know . . .'

The change that came over Erich's face was dramatic. She had clearly touched upon a very raw spot, yet there was more confusion and embarrassment in his face than pain. Fiona could only guess the reasons behind his discomfort for he quickly changed the subject, entreating her to tell him about her working life in England.

Mentally shrugging the incident aside, Fiona complied. After all, many, many men had reason to associate unhappy memories with nurses. There were a great many nurses in the world, and by far the majority were young and unmarried . . .

For an hour Fiona talked freely about her life in Elchester, the operating theatre at St Helen's—everything, in fact, except Daniel Davenport. She left him firmly out of the conversation. She did not fancy putting herself in the unfortunate position into which she had inadvertently plunged Erich earlier in their talk.

'But St Helen's all seems a long way from here,' she sighed eventually, 'and I don't think I'm going to want to leave here one little bit. I've only got another one and a half weeks and that will go even faster than the days have gone so far, and then it'll be back to Elchester . . . Uggh!' she grimaced to underline her feelings.

'Come and work here in Switzerland,' Erich invited with an expansive gesture.

'Oh, thank you for your kind offer,' Fiona grinned at him. 'And you'll just fix me up with a job, will you?'

Erich smiled sheepishly.

'Just an idea,' he shrugged.

'You know what I think of your ideas!' Fiona responded.

She paid the bill in spite of Erich's protests. It was not such an unusual thing for her to do, had he but known it, and she liked the idea that she was back on an equal footing with him.

She refused, too, his offer to accompany her home. The walk back to the hotel was not far, and she wanted to be alone to think. It was not yet late.

All her reserves of physical and mental energy had been used up for today. Each evening Fiona had wondered at the way skiing did this for her, knowing that this was what real relaxation meant. She had always felt that theatre nursing performed the same function, whereas caring for patients on the wards had always left her physically exhausted with her mind still buzzing.

She found her mind wandering back now to Erich's strange reaction to her light remark about nurses. She wondered momentarily whether she had been rude, but quickly dismissed the idea. No, he had been embarrassed, guilty even. But that was not her affair. She smiled to herself at her own pun.

Her own affairs were beginning to fall into perspective, she realised. She felt less and less pain when, on odd occasions, Daniel's face appeared in her mind. In fact, she felt more and more healthily indignant at his behaviour towards her. It seemed that men had ceased to play an important part in her life . . . well, almost. She still had to banish a certain strong profile, a deep, concerned voice from the depths of a Mercedes. But she was doing her best to eliminate them from her memory, and her best was all that she could possibly do.

Fiona got up, showered and dressed in a fresh red and white ribbed sweater and her ski suit. It was Friday, and the end of the first week of her holiday.

She piled her hair up and pulled her white hat over the shining topknot, and then she looked at herself in the mirror. To her amazement, she had actually managed to acquire a light tan on her face—a very unusual achievement for her. She did not have the freckles which normally characterised her hair colouring, but she paid the price of an even fairer, finer skin than other redheads had. The subtle change she now saw made her turquoise eyes seem even deeper blue, her hair appear even more aflame.

This was proving to be the most marvellous holiday of her life, Fiona decided, as she walked through the almost deserted early morning streets of the village. Around her she was aware of the orderly lives of the real inhabitants of Wengen. One or two village women were already carrying shopping back from the grocery stores to their hidden houses in narrow back streets. Here, each householder looked in upon his neighbour, so close were their shuttered windows and sheltered balconies festooned with washing.

A black-capped, wizened old man passed Fiona and nodded a quiet greeting to her, and she found herself wondering how long it would take for an outsider to become accepted in a village such as this. She was thinking not of the passing tourists, but of other residents—such as the couple in the mountainside house. She wondered whether each woodcutter and shopkeeper knew and accepted them as well as the station-master and the tobacconist seemed to have done. For she felt certain that the man had not been born here.

Erich had instructed Fiona to meet him at lunch-time. She was to ski the lower slopes alone this morning and report to him to tell him how she had coped with them. It was an exciting challenge and Fiona filled her mind with the tips and warnings that he had instilled into her during their week of intensive lessons. She was determined to prove to him her ability.

It was good to find that she was among the first to arrive at the nursery slopes. When she had satisfied herself that she could ski these effortlessly, she took a chair-lift up to the next group of *pistes* and practised on these until lunch-time. She could feel herself improving and it was a wonderful feeling.

But her euphoria was banished by the crush in the restaurant at lunch-time. She could barely hear herself think and she cursed Erich for telling her to meet him at peak time.

'How did you get on?' he asked.

Fiona, who had taken nearly half an hour to collect and pay for her salad at the self-service counter, was greatly irritated to see Erich's empty plate and beer glass.

'Fine. I think,' she snapped. 'I didn't fall once,' she added.

'It doesn't seem to have been good for your humour, to ski alone!' Erich joked.

Fiona put her tray down and clicked her tongue in annoyance. 'It's this place . . . I'm hungry.'

'Well, eat then. I was going to suggest that you might care to do that wooded descent to the village that you have so much admired from afar . . .'

'With you?' Fiona had said, before she realised how rude her remark might sound.

'No. Alone. I have a new pupil, if I am free.'

'I see.'

Fiona did see. She saw a raven-haired beauty who was currently giving Erich an extremely appreciative look over her glass of *Glühwein*.

'I would love to do it alone, Erich,' Fiona told him, slightly put out, but not much surprised by his fickleness. 'Do you think I can cope with it all right?'

'Why not?' her instructor replied. 'You have experience enough, but you must be careful. It is not so steep, but there is always fresh snow over the track left by the caterpillar tractor. It falls from the tree. This is dangerous. So you must keep your eyes, how do you say, peeled?'

Fiona smiled.

'I will take great care. I promise. I am very sensible,' she said.

'Yes. I know all about that,' Erich said, looking hard at her.

Far too sensible to have got involved with you, Fiona was thinking. The same old charm, the same old fickleness that she had seen before in Daniel. Perhaps she was truly learning at last.

'Shall I see you over the weekend?' Erich asked.

There was nothing like keeping all options open.

'No,' Fiona responded firmly. 'Monday morning for our lesson. Goodbye, Erich.'

She got up and made for the doors of the restaurant.

She had to fight to disentangle her skis from the mass that had been placed in the rack since she had stopped for lunch. The hubbub from the restaurant still reached her outside, and the prospect of a silent, solitary run down into the village, leaving all the other skiers up here on the intermediate *pistes*, appealed more and more to Fiona.

The pine trees at the mouth of the path scented the crisp air with their delicate fragrance and here and there the sun broke through the thick trees and sparkled on the snow on either side of the track. The peace and tranquillity of the hidden descent was to be her secret reward for the week's hard work behind her.

She stood for a moment or two, savouring the prospect of it, and then set off slowly, the silence of her snowy path broken only by the soft swish of her skis. She felt as though she were flying; as if she was free for the first time in her life from all the restraints that her body put upon her. She swerved gently from side to side on the little path as she moved downhill, controlling her speed so that she could enjoy every minute of the descent.

She had been skiing gently down through the trees for about twenty minutes when she fell. She did so slowly, almost as if in slow motion, and before she had realised what was happening she was lying in a crumpled heap in the snow, her skis twisted painfully beneath her.

She stared, dazed, at the rut which had caused her fall; a deep depression in the path, covered by a light drift of fresh snow. It was exactly what Erich had warned her of. There was a small and, until now, invisible, mound of stones in the rut which had diverted her right ski from its course. Fiona applied her mind to trying to remember what she should do in such a situation.

She tried to get both ankles side by side across the slope, so that she would be able to stand up, but it was no good. There was no way in which she could turn her right ankle in order to set it straight. Cursing softly under her breath, Fiona unclipped the safety strap and tried to get her boot out of its binding on the right ski. The pain that shot up her thigh told her not to try to move that foot again.

Panic took hold of her, and it was even more paralysing than the pain in her right ankle. She did up the safety strap once more to stop the ski from sliding away. There had been plenty of things that had worried Fiona about coming away on this skiing holiday, but the old cliché of a broken leg had simply not been among them. Now she realised that even that might turn out to be the least of her problems.

Erich had told her again and again when she had drawn his attention to this tempting path, how little used it was. She was now a good two kilometres from the crowded intermediate *pistes* where skiers were enjoying the last of the afternoon sunshine. She had been late beginning her run down to the village, thanks to the congestion in the restaurant at lunch-time, and the light was already beginning to fade. Fiona knew that even if she were to shout at the top of her voice, nobody would hear her call.

She sat very still and tried to order her thoughts. Meanwhile, she became more and more aware of the cold reaching up around her, threatening her with its barely perceptible dulling of the senses. She knew how terribly easy it was to slip into sleep, and then into coma.

Her foot was almost completely numb now. The sun was sinking behind the far mountains, lengthening and deepening the shadows cast across the path by the trees.

Darkness would soon replace the inky gloom of the mountain track, and she would be really lost. Her only hope was to try to get to the village, which she reckoned was half-an-hour's walk away. But it would take much longer than that to crawl there.

She tried to move down the slope, but after a couple of feet was forced to stop by the pain in her ankle. The silence of the mountains seemed to close around her in the gathering darkness, and Fiona began to feel really afraid. She shut her eyes momentarily, trying to control her panic.

The sound of muffled footsteps broke in upon her and she opened her eyes again, terrified, struggling to make out the origin of the sounds. To her mixed horror and relief, she saw the large figure of a man coming steadily down the track towards her. He seemed simultaneously to catch sight of her, and to quicken his pace towards the huddled figure in his path.

Fiona held her breath while tears of fear gathered behind her eyelids. The man stopped beside her and Fiona pushed her cuff roughly across her eyes to clear her vision. She met the face that had haunted her thoughts ever since she had first seen it. There could be no doubt of the identity of her rescuer.

The man did not say a word. He expertly undid her skis and stacked them against a tree just off the path, and then he swept Fiona up off the snow and she felt the material of his anorak and inhaled the faint smell of his tobacco. Then she knew nothing but the safety of his strong arms about her.

When she came to, Fiona was sure that she was dreaming. She seemed to be in a modern medical surgery or clinic treatment room, lying on an examination couch.

'Where are we?' she asked in a voice which did not sound like her own at all.

'In my clinic,' came the brisk reply. Fiona blinked. Her benefactor was washing his hands at a basin nearby. He was in his shirt sleeves.

'Your clinic?' she repeated stupidly.

'What on earth were you doing, skiing that path alone?' he asked, irritation in his voice. 'And how long had you been lying there? You could quite easily have remained there all night before you were found.'

'Yes. I mean, thank you,' Fiona began haltingly. 'I don't know how long . . .'

'Idiotic thing to do,' the doctor pronounced.

Fiona formed the impression that he had decided that she was not worth conversing with over this issue, and that this last remark had been self-addressed.

But he was working skilfully to remove the two pairs of socks that she was wearing, to compare her two feet and to examine carefully the injured one. Fiona winced only once, when he gently twisted her right foot to determine the extent of injury to the ankle. Otherwise, she discovered his touch to be sure, gentle, firm and practised. He tested each toe for numbness and mobility and Fiona was pleased to find that, in spite of the pain, she could move everything. At least she had not broken anything.

'You are a very lucky young woman,' the doctor told her in a voice that suggested he did not think she deserved her luck. He looked severely put out.

'It's not broken, then?' Fiona ventured.

'It is not. But the foot is badly sprained. The Achilles tendon is injured and there will be no more skiing for you—for a few days anyway,' he announced. He gave his verdict in tones which suggested resignation to the stupidity of skiers.

'Can I get down off this?' Fiona asked. She felt suddenly at a disadvantage lying on the couch. And it crossed her mind that the doctor might be a little more gracious, as this was presumably the way in which he earned his income.

The doctor shrugged in answer to her question. Fiona edged herself into a sitting position and swung her legs down off the couch. Supporting herself with straight arms on either side of her knees, she felt exactly the way she remembered feeling after a medical exam at school. Her feeling was reinforced by the refusal of her rescuer to treat her like an adult.

'Have you any idea how much of my time I waste on self-induced injuries, or of the sheer stupidity of some skiers?' he asked indifferently.

'No,' said Fiona sharply. She did not care, either.

She did not know whether it was the long day behind her, delayed reaction to her fear on the mountain path, pain or the misery that this doctor seemed to want to put her through, but she suddenly felt very close to tears.

'About ninety per cent of my time,' he informed her coldly. He took out his gold pen, and held it delicately between the forefingers of both hands. He studied it and then looked up at his patient on the couch. Fiona glanced hastily down at her rapidly swelling foot.

'Do I buy a support bandage and keep it elevated then?' she asked.

'Precisely.' The doctor's exclamation was rich with sarcasm. 'Very good indeed. So you learned some first aid before coming on your skiing holiday. Very commendable.'

He smiled triumphantly. He appeared to be enjoying himself immensely at Fiona's expense.

Something snapped inside her. So this was the other side of the cool character who had shared her train compartment, greeted his children so adoringly and offered her a lift so chivalrously the other evening!

'No,' she pronounced slowly and carefully, 'I did not

learn some first aid. As a matter of fact, I did not have to
do so. It happens that I am a nursing sister in charge of an
operating theatre in a very reputable British hospital
where patients are treated with a good deal more respect
than they appear to command here in Switzerland . . .
or, at least, in Wengen.'

Fiona shocked herself by saying much more than she
had meant to say, but she had the satisfaction of watching the doctor's back straighten slightly at her words.
The effect was subtle, but unmistakable.

'I do beg your pardon,' he said quietly.

'Thank you,' Fiona returned.

It was with horror that she realised the effect of his
apology. The hot tears, which had been arrested by her
angry outburst, now began their inevitable course down
her cheeks in burning streams.

The doctor got to his feet and came slowly over to the
examination couch. He placed one arm coolly around
Fiona's shoulders and pulled her towards him so that he
took most of her weight as she lowered herself gingerly
to the floor. He helped her to hop to a chair near his desk
and he placed a stool in front of her, on to which Fiona
obediently lifted her foot. His action had shocked her
tears into abeyance.

'I want you to sit still there while I do something about
this ankle,' he told her firmly. 'I shall apply a support
bandage. I shall not leave it to you—in spite of your
undoubted qualification,' he added quickly. And then,
in a lower tone, 'If you will forgive the observation, in
my experience nurses do not always make the most
proficient bandagers.'

Fiona waited in silence for the doctor to bring a
bandage from a side-room. She could think of no apt
reply to this last remark. For it was true that she, for one,
was an abysmally poor bandager. She had tried and
failed to master the art in preliminary training school,

and her weakness had followed her throughout her otherwise shining career as a nurse.

She had no option but to sit and look meekly down at the shiny crown of dark hair above the broad shoulders while her rescuer expertly bound up her ankle. When he had finished the result was immaculate.

'Given that you do your own bandaging,' Fiona began with a small smile, 'don't you have a nurse to help you in the clinic? Or do you have the only nurse in the world who can apply a bandage . . . ?'

Fiona stopped short at the change that came over the doctor's features. He was following her gaze with a frown. In the side-room, Fiona could see stacks of plaster of Paris dressings, rolls of Tubegauz and other accoutrements which she associated purely with the nursing end of orthopaedic care.

'I do not have nursing help,' the doctor told her. His mouth was a hard line. 'Now, move your toes.'

She did so, and then watched while he resumed his seat behind the desk.

'I assume that your young man does not know where you are?' he enquired. Fiona could feel the change in his attitude towards her, and she traced it back to her last remark. She could not understand how she could have offended him.

'Young man? Erich is just my ski instructor,' Fiona said calmly. But she suddenly felt the colour rising to her cheeks. The scene outside the night-club returned to her with painful clarity. 'No, he does not know where I am,' she finished miserably.

The doctor scanned Fiona's face.

'Your ski instructor,' he said, articulating each word precisely, 'needs some tuition himself. Why did he let you go off on your own?'

'He did not *let* me,' Fiona almost shouted. 'I wanted to ski on my own. He judged me capable. That is what I

came here for—to be on my own.' She had got carried
away again, and again she had said more than she had
meant to say.

'Ah! So that is why you go dancing into the early hours
of the morning with your, er, ski instructor?' The words
were laden with insinuation.

Fiona had fallen into her own trap. She felt a hundred
emotions flood through her in the next seconds. She
thought of a hundred things she wanted to say. But a
sudden weariness had come over her. She no longer
cared what he thought, or how he misconstrued things.
She did not matter to him and nothing about her life
would ever be of any significance to him. Why should she
worry?

'Now, what is your name?' the doctor asked her
formally. His pen was poised above an official-looking
form.

'Fiona Shore,' Fiona said stiffly.

Looking up every few moments with a dispassionate
expression, the doctor elicited from Fiona her age, her
date of birth, her nationality and her professional
status—for the second time—as well as brief details
of her uneventful medical history. Fiona answered his
questions in a flat voice.

She wished with all her soul that none of this afternoon had happened. All her innermost imaginings had
been reduced to cold, cruel reality. Skiing that forest
trail had come to symbolise her independence and all her
aspirations had come crashing to the ground with her on
that snowy path. And of all the people to witness at first
hand her utter humiliation, fate had sent this man. It had
been bad enough to know that outside her life there
existed one for whom she longed within it; sad enough to
know that he would continue to live outside her reality.
But this . . . this was too cruel.

The doctor thought her incapable of ordering her

own existence and she seemed incapable of doing anything to redeem herself in his eyes. She found herself cursing Erich for not being around on the one occasion when she had really needed him.

'Fine,' the doctor said. He put his pen down deliberately on the desk and ran his fingers through his thick, dark hair as if he were alone in his consulting room at the end of a busy day.

'Have you finished with me?' Fiona asked.

'Oh, I shouldn't think so for a moment,' he casually replied. He came and helped her to her feet once more and remained beside her, his hand under her elbow. 'I think I'd better drive you home, don't you?'

'That would be very kind of you,' Fiona murmured.

The doctor took a sheepskin coat down from a hook behind the door and then he led her out of the surgery, turning the lights off behind them as they went.

The reception area at the front of the clinic was and impressive. Decorated with masses of green pot plants, it was dominated by a long reception desk topped by a fleet of important-looking red telephones. A marble-topped table matched the fine slabs of marble that made up the floor, and provided ample space for magazines and coffee cups for waiting patients and relatives. Framed prints of low-flying aircraft in mountain scenery adorned the walls, and Fiona took everything in breathlessly.

'What a beautiful place this is,' she exclaimed, carried away by her surroundings.

'Thank you,' the doctor said simply.

'Do you have many staff?'

'Myself and two medical assistants,' the doctor replied. 'But there are many volunteers. All the best skiers in the village—I think your, er, instructor, is among them, do the main work of bringing casualties in from the mountains. They find them, give them emergency treatment and then bring them down to us by ski or light aircraft. Sometimes they work in appalling weather conditions. After that, my work is fairly straightforward.' He gave Fiona a crooked smile, the first that she had seen that was not ambivalent. As he did so he ushered her out of the clinic and locked the main doors.

'I'd never have thought of all that,' Fiona said truthfully. It all seemed so far removed from her own clinical world. She could hardly believe that all this drama was going on while she quietly took cases in General Theatre One at St Helen's Hospital.

She was helped into the comfortable front seat of the Mercedes and sank into the upholstery with a sense of unreality.

'Are there a lot of accidents during the skiing season?' She tried to keep her voice steady, but she could hardly do so in this situation. She wanted to look at the man beside her, to savour the moment forever.

'Yes. We are extremely busy. People are, it is true, over-confident on skis.'

'Yes,' Fiona said in a chastened voice. 'I can accept that.'

An unmistakable smile softened the profile next to her.

'If you are really interested professionally, I can show you how we work here,' he offered in neutral tones. Fiona stiffened. He started the engine of the car and the Mercedes slid away from the clinic in the direction of the centre of the village.

'I would very much like to see anything you can show me,' Fiona said. But her enthusiasm must have been evident behind the formality of her response, for the doctor took his eyes briefly from the road to glance at her with quiet amusement.

'You are very involved with your work, Sister? That is your title in England?'

'Yes. Yes, I do like my work very much. Perhaps I had forgotten just how much until just now, in your clinic.'

'And you return soon to Britian?'

Fiona watched the profile next to her as it was lit by the lights of an oncoming car.

'No. Not until the end of next week. I was hoping to get another full week skiing. I am just a beginner,' she added modestly.

'You will be able to ski by the end of next week, or even by the middle, if you are sensible. Where is your hotel?'

Fiona directed him and soon, too soon, the Mercedes crept up the drive. The doctor got out first and came round to open her door for her.

'I can manage, honestly, thank you.' Fiona tried to refuse the arm that was extended to her, but when she did so the doctor firmly took hold of her own and helped up to the door.

'I always seem to be thanking you,' Fiona faltered.

She rang the door bell rather than search for her keys under the scrutiny of this disturbing man.

He was standing very close to her; so close that she could feel his warm breath in her hair.

He handed her a small white card which she took with trembling fingers.

'Call me, or come by taxi, Miss Shore. Come to-morrow. It is always a good time to see how we work, over the weekend. We are always busy on a Saturday. Goodnight.'

'Goodnight,' Fiona whispered as she heard the land-lady opening the door from the inside. Before it was open the Mercedes and its driver had disappeared.

Fiona found that she could put her foot down without too much pain, and she gratefully followed the landlady into the cosy dining-room where she was promised hot chocolate and freshly baked appleflap. The cuckoo clock told her that the time was only half-past six, but she felt as though it was midnight.

She held her hands out to the fire and suddenly recalled the card she had been given. She could not remember which pocket she had put it in, and for a moment feared that she must have dropped it in the snow outside the front door. But, after a frantic search, she found it in one of her anorak pockets.

She tried to read the embossed card, but the only words that made sense to her were *dr Hans Eckhart*. She could also distinguish the address and telephone number of the clinic and another, presumably his home, address. The doctor evidently stopped short of taking business calls at home. The card had the simplicity of something expensively produced. Fiona thought it odd that the foreign abbreviation for 'doctor' should employ no capital letters, but if there seemed to be a touching modesty about this, there had certainly been nothing self-effacing about Dr Eckhart.

He had possessed all the superiority of his British counterparts at consultant level, Fiona mused. But she was thrilled at the prospect of looking further at the way the clinic worked. She told herself that she would be less willing to accept critical remarks about the competence of nurses while on her official tour. After all, she would be visiting as a professional. Her mind flashed back to his strange response to her question about nursing help. Never mind, perhaps all would become clear tomorrow.

Anyway, one thing was certain, the very thought of tomorrow made her heart turn over as thoroughly as the pastry had been flipped over the clove-scented apples in the appleflap which the landlady presently set before her. And it was not simply her first sip of chocolate that sent the blood coursing hotly through her veins . . .

CHAPTER FOUR

FIONA could not put her finger on what exactly it was that unsettled her about the Weiss Kreuz Klinik. She stirred her coffee mechanically and stared hard at a vast and spectacular specimen of Mother-in-law's Tongue which adorned the marble coffee table top. It was eleven o'clock in the morning and the clinic was buzzing around her.

She had been here for two hours already. Dr Eckhart had turned up at her hotel promptly at nine, just as she was sitting over the last of her breakfast and worrying about making herself understood on the telephone to the taxi-rank. In fact, she had practically decided not to try, but to hobble down the road instead, in the hope that a taxi would pass, stop and take her to the clinic.

The landlady had seemed impressed by the appearance of the doctor at her hotel and had approached Fiona with a respectful air to tell her that he had arrived for her. Taken completely by surprise, Fiona had mercifully escaped the worst of the anxiety and nervousness that had been building up inside her at the prospect of the day ahead.

Nevertheless, the sight of Dr Eckhart had been enough to throw her into inner confusion during the short journey from the dining-room into the hall, and she was trembling by the time he took her coat from her arm and held it for her to slip into.

'It is kind of you to come for me,' she had murmured. 'I fear that a night's rest has done my foot more harm than good; it's very stiff and sore this morning.'

'That is very often the case with bad sprains. It will, I

think, improve as the day goes on,' he had commented drily.

The drive to the clinic had passed quickly and Fiona had realised for the first time where it stood in relation to the rest of the village. It was on the fork of the road leading up from the station towards the forest—the one which avoided the village centre and at the top of which was the beautiful house.

The clinic, above which proudly flew the Swiss flag—the white cross on a scarlet ground after which the clinic was named—looked even more imposing by daylight.

Passing through the double doors behind Dr Eckhart, she had again felt the warm air of the reception hall embrace her cold cheeks, but this time she had acknowledged a welcoming smile from a pretty blonde receptionist.

Dr Eckhart had introduced her formally as a British nursing sister, using her surname only, and she had noted with some surprise and a small flush of pleasure the raised eyebrows and obvious interest shown by the doctor's young medical assistant in response to this information. Dr Wilhelm was clearly most interested in the workings of the British National Health Service, and was keen to assure Fiona that the British system was the envy of the world.

Fiona had been able to answer most, if not all, his questions, but had been somewhat relieved when the young physician had been called away to see a patient. It was good to sit down with a cup of coffee and have a moment to take stock of her situation.

Last night, in the silent and deserted clinic, Fiona had formed an impression of it as a compact, smallish set-up with rather limited resources. Now she realised that connecting doors had hidden the bulk of the place from her view, and this morning the clinic had opened up into something like an out-patients department.

She had been shown no less than four treatment rooms, one of which was reserved for minor surgery and set up as a miniature operating theatre, complete with table and operating lamp. In addition, she had toured a plaster room, an X-ray room and a general treatment room.

Each treatment/consulting room had its own documentation desk, examination couch, wash-basin and medicine cupboard, as well as a store-room off it for general supplies. It was these that had unsettled Fiona. As a nurse she had a highly-developed sense of order, and her attention had been arrested by the state of the cupboards in the clinic.

In her nursing experience Fiona had encountered many doctors whose orderliness of mind had been amply demonstrated in the neatness of their case-note entries, and yet this quality had rarely, if ever, been reflected in their practical work. Fiona pondered now as she had done often before upon this inconsistency.

It seemed that a doctor, while he could follow a perfectly methodical pattern while examining a patient, hardly ever bothered to devise a simple, tidy way of organising his own working space. Fiona had dismissed a sexist explanation when she had discovered that female doctors were as bad as their male counterparts!

But perhaps nurses were responsible for the muddled way in which doctors worked. Nurses were forever laying up trolleys for doctors, tidying up after doctors and generally making their lives easy for them . . .

'Will you take some more coffee?' Renata was standing in front of her, coffee-pot in hand. 'Dr Eckhart will be back shortly. He has just telephoned to me.'

The senior doctor had been called urgently home on a domestic matter and had gone off in his car some half-hour ago. Since then, Fiona had been aware of the receptionist's concern for her well-being and had been grateful for it.

'So. You are being looked after?'

Dr Eckhart's voice echoed her thoughts. His tall figure beside her made Fiona want automatically to stand up, but before she could do so, the doctor had taken a seat next to her. Leaning forward slightly in the low chair, as if unaccustomed to the comfort which it afforded, Fiona noticed his features softening. She formed an immediate and strong impression that the interruption to his working morning had not been welcome and that he was glad to be back in the clinic. Renata set a cup of coffee down in front of him.

'She has been most kind,' Fiona said.

The doctor nodded absent-mindedly.

'Almost time for lunch,' he briskly announced. 'But first I have to see to one or two things.' He finished his coffee quickly. 'Will you come through while I clear things up?' he invited.

It was one thing to listen to a foreigner with perfect command of the English language; another to hear him employ colloquialisms like a native. Fiona found herself thrown more and more off guard by the cool charm of her host.

She allowed herself to be ushered through into the same treatment room with which she had become familiar under such different circumstances last night.

The doctor sat down at the desk and immediately immersed himself in his paperwork. Fiona was left quietly and discreetly looking about her. He glanced up momentarily and gestured towards a chair, as if suddenly aware of her standing there, and she nodded and smiled her thanks. But instead of sitting down, she wandered casually over towards the store-room and stood looking in through the open door.

She let her gaze wander slowly over the shelves. The

neat stacks of supplies were all labelled in a meticulous hand: elastic bandages—*elastische Binden*; splints—*Schienen*; plaster of Paris bandages—*Gips Binden* and sticking plaster, marked *Heftpflaster*. Fiona, her back carefully turned on Dr Eckhart, stood in thought.

It was these quiet, unobstrusive labels that had been bothering her. But why? She recalled the sprawling handwriting on the case sheet that he had made out for her last night. No. These labels had been written by a woman.

She thought of Renata and searched her memory for a visual image of the memos that had littered the reception desk that morning but, try as she might, she could not recall the receptionist's handwriting.

Yet she was certain that the hand that had written these labels was the same one that was behind the long-established order of the clinic and, almost by instinct, she recognised the hand of one of her own profession. There had been a nurse here. Yet the doctor had denied it.

'I am ready, Miss Shore,' said Dr Eckhart, and Fiona realised with a small shock that he was standing directly behind her. 'What are you finding of such great interest in there? May I ask?'

'Oh, nothing really. Nothing at all,' Fiona stammered, overcome with embarrassment at the interruption of her thoughts. 'I was just thinking how very well-organised everything is,' she finished lamely, if truthfully.

'You are most complimentary,' he said. 'And now I shall buy you some lunch to sustain you for the afternoon in this rather well-organised place.'

Fiona followed the doctor out of the consulting room and back into the subdued atmosphere of the reception hall. On a sudden impulse, she excused herself from him and crossed to the desk. Renata looked up from the message that she was writing and Fiona saw her clear,

large handwriting. She wondered how she could have
failed to remember it. It was quite different from the
neat, compact italic lettering of the shelf labels.

'Thank you for looking after me so well this morning,
Renata,' Fiona said.

'*Bitte*. You are most welcome,' the receptionist responded with a smile.

Fiona rejoined Dr Eckhart and together they left the
clinic. The Mercedes purred through the centre of the
village and out along a road which Fiona did not recognise. They drove uphill in silence for some distance and
arrived fifteen minutes later at a secluded chalet situated
quite high above the village. The doctor again got out
of the car and once more came around to help Fiona
out.

He took her arm and helped her across the snow to the
porch of the chalet where they were met by a pleasant-
faced elderly woman wearing an immaculate white lace
apron. She opened an inner door and Fiona was drawn
into one of the prettiest dining-rooms that she had ever
seen. Red and white checked table-cloths matched curtains which framed the snowscapes outside and a log fire
burned brightly in the iron grate. It was reflected in the
copper pots and pans which surrounded the fireplace.

To add to the perfection, the place was full of fresh
flowers. But best of all, it was deserted apart from themselves and the woman who owned it. Fiona sat at the
high bar and accepted a glass of sparkling mineral water
while Dr Eckhart waited for his glass of wine. He had
ordered their drinks with the same thought and care with
which he seemed to do everything else, and Fiona felt his
composure convey itself to her and have a calming effect
upon her.

She responsed easily and readily to his questions.

'It is a very different set-up from the one which you are
used to?' he enquired of the clinic.

'Yes,' Fiona responded, replacing her glass on the shining bar. 'Very different.'

'And do you enjoy theatre work?'

'I do.' Fiona replied thoughtfully, 'but I sometimes find it rather isolating. One sees so little of the rest of the hospital or of the rest of the staff. Perhaps it makes one a little inward-looking.'

'Quite so.'

Before she had had time to check herself, Fiona found that she had begun to voice her own feelings about his clinic.

'I do find it surprising that you do not employ a nurse . . .' but she was arrested mid-sentence by the expression which she found on his face.

'And what makes you say that?' he enquired, his voice hard.

'Well,' Fiona went on nervously, 'I can see so many ways in which the running of the clinic might go more smoothly had you a nursing sister.'

The doctor held her fixed by his stare, as if challenging her to continue, and however hard she wished that she had never begun this conversation, Fiona had no alternative but to go on with it. It felt like a walk to the gallows.

'For example,' she continued warily, 'this morning I saw Dr Wilhelm bandaging a shoulder while a cast was setting in the other room. I mean, it is so crucial to check the plaster as it gets hard and one can miss the point of no return so easily. If you had a nurse . . .'

'. . . she may be capable of neither task,' the doctor pronounced forcefully and bitterly. The tension caused between them hung in the air like a summer thunder storm.

Fiona, dismayed as she was by her own forwardness, was determined not to be too submissive under professional attack.

'That is probably an unfair comment,' she said, softly and with dignity.

'You must expect them if you continue to consider the staffing of the clinic your concern,' the doctor replied angrily.

'Yes. I do beg your pardon,' Fiona said. She meant it.

There was a long silence during which he finished his wine and ordered a second glass, and Fiona stared unhappily into her own empty glass and refused more water. Why was he so touchy about nurses and yet so hospitable to her? It did not make sense. But perhaps he had offered her this day out of courtesy and was already regretting his charity. Fiona was filled with hopeless confusion and discomfort. She made up her mind to get quietly through the afternoon without allowing herself the smallest remark upon the subject that she now knew she must avoid. After all, the doctor was right. It really was none of her business why he didn't employ a nurse.

A more easy atmosphere between them established itself as they sat down to a delicious selection of salads and cold meats and then hot, home-made appleflap.

Back in the car, Fiona felt herself fighting off the conflicting feelings that she seemed to experience all the time she was with this man, while beside her the doctor appeared to be concentrating all his attention upon the snowy downhill road. She looked at his motionless profile and sighed.

'I hope that you do not sigh in dissatisfaction?' he asked her in a cool voice.

'No. Not at all. It was a lovely lunch,' Fiona replied quickly.

He seemed to be able to read her all too well.

One obviously female patient was screaming, and another was crying. Dr Eckhart had his coat off before they had crossed the reception area and, for once, Fiona was left to remove her own. There was no sign of Dr Willhelm, and Renata was not at her desk.

The reception area was full of people, many in ski clothing, and Fiona instantly recognised Erich among them. He looked at her with obvious surprise at finding her here, and the worried frown on his face lifted fleetingly.

'Fiona! What are you doing here?'

His gaze travelled down and alighted on her bandaged ankle.

'You are all right?'

'Oh, yes,' Fiona replied ironically, 'I am just fine. What are *you* doing here?'

Erich had had time only to shrug in preparation for his answer when Fiona's attention was diverted from him by the sudden appearance of both Dr Eckhart and his receptionist. She caught the end of his remark to Renata— '. . . *Narkose*. But she did not need to have heard any more than that. Renata had picked up one of the red telephones and was summoning an anaesthetist.

'Miss Shore!'

Dr Eckhart's voice was steely with professional preoccupation. He gestured to her and she followed him quickly into the treatment room. He flung her a white coat and she put it on and crossed automatically to the basin to wash her hands. She seemed to be obeying an instinctive professional response from deep within herself.

While she washed, she looked through the connecting doors to a second consulting room where she could just see the figure of a young girl lying on the examination couch. It was her screams that had greeted Fiona and Dr Eckhart upon their return from lunch, but now she lay quietly.

Fiona was unable to see her injuries from where she

stood, but the very stillness of the patient was enough to convince her of their seriousness.

Fiona turned her attention to the patient, who lay on the same examination couch which she herself had occupied last night. She finished drying her hands and crossed quietly to the couch. With a shock, she recognised the plump brunette whom she had seen with Erich in the ski shop soon after her arrival in Wengen. Now the girl lay with her eyes closed, beads of sweat accumulating on her pale forehead.

Fiona took her wrist and registered the cold clammy skin of the shocked patient. The pulse was typically weak, rapid and thready. Fiona quickly found the mechanism by which she could lower the head of the examination couch, and did so.

The girl's trouser leg had been slit open along its length to allow the application of an aluminium splint. The rescuers must have suspected a fracture.

As Fiona took the sphygmomanometer down from the wall to measure the blood pressure, the girl opened her eyes briefly, but closed them again without apparently recognising Fiona. The blood pressure measured a hundred over sixty millimetres of mercury—low, but not dangerously low.

Fiona found a clean case note sheet and recorded the measurements that she had made, glanced quickly at her patient once more, and went briskly through to report her findings to Dr Eckhart.

'Get Wilhelm to X-ray her and let me know if she sinks any deeper into shock. This one will have to be stitched under a general because of the eye injuries . . .'

Fiona looked quickly at the white face of the girl and assessed the lid lacerations and other cuts beneath the blood-matted hairline. The cuts looked deep, black and clean—as if they had been inflicted with a knife.

Dr Wilhelm entered the room and said something in

rapid German to Dr Eckhart, who told Fiona that he was going to check the operating room in preparation for his patient. In the meantime he would like her to have injections of anti-tetanus toxoid and an antibiotic.

Dr Wilhelm began examining the brunette while Fiona found syringes, needles and went to the fridge to find Ampicillin and toxoid. The injured girl seemed too ill even to notice Fiona gently rolling her to one side and administering the drugs.

Fiona experienced a sense of professional relief when Dr Wilhelm came and took her into the operating room, leaving the brunette once more under her care.

She resumed her place at the head of the first couch and repeated her pulse and blood pressure recordings. The BP had risen by ten millimetres of mercury on both the systolic and the diastolic readings, and Fiona could see an improvement in the patient.

'Hello, don't I know you?'

The girl had opened her eyes and was staring at Fiona in obvious confusion.

'Yes,' she reassured her, 'we met briefly at the ski shop. You were with Erich, trying on some new boots.'

'And look where they landed me!'

The girl tried to smile, and then her expression changed to one of worry and fear.

'How is Sue?' she asked.

'Is that the name of the other girl?' Fiona asked.

'Yes. It was terrible . . .' The brunette closed her eyes for a second, as if remembering. 'We'd gone down alone. Erich said we should be able to manage it . . . and then I fell. I don't know exactly how it happened, and then Sue was lying there, and my skis had hit her head . . . it was dreadful . . .'

A chill ran down Fiona's spine. Damn Erich, she thought with a stab of fury. She took her patient's hand. Tears were pouring down her white cheeks.

'Don't think about it any more,' Fiona said softly. 'Everything will be all right. The doctors are stitching her now and she will be okay.'

'I hope so,' sobbed the brunette. 'I don't know why I came skiing at all. It's all my fault. I never got the hang of it, and now this . . .'

'But you must't blame yourself,' Fiona insisted gently, and with feeling. 'It's the easiest thing in the world to fall while skiing. Even the best skiers do so—quite often. You must try to rest and relax.'

It was three-quarters of an hour later that Dr Wilhelm eventually reappeared, his mask still around his neck from the operation. He immediately got X-rays taken, satisfied himself that there was no fracture and applied a support bandage to the leg. Apparently, the operation to stitch the lid lacerations and other facial cuts was going well, and would be over soon.

With her patient taken from her, Fiona felt suddenly redundant. She registered her own aching ankle with displeasure, slipped off her white coat and thought about going back to her comfortable hotel room with growing tiredness. She was pleased to see Renata's cheerful smile and to accept her offer of coffee. She had begun to feel as if the day was too long.

But the clock in the reception area said only four-thirty, and in the last of the afternoon sunlight Fiona could see skiers returning from the slopes. She had forgotten already how work could distort time!

She felt a light touch on her shoulder and turned to meet Erich's serious face.

'How are they?' he asked.

Fiona detected the guilt behind his question and, thinking of her patient's tear-stained face, had a sudden desire to hurt the ski instructor.

'You really shouldn't ask me,' she replied icily instead. 'I am in no position to tell you anything. But I

believe that Dr Eckhart is almost finished with your
client, and I'm sure that he will speak to you when he is
ready.'

Her feelings were painfully clear to Erich, who
winced. It served him right, Fiona thought. She was
swiftly forming a mental compartment for men like him.

Watching Renata quietly tidying up in the consulting
rooms, confirming her suspicion that it was she who
maintained order here in place of a nurse, Fiona thought
about all the little things that had struck her while she
had been working herself today.

Little things like the absence of proper disposal
methods for used needles and broken glass; a fridge that
needed defrosting and some disorder among the drugs
that were kept chilled in there, too. It was as if the
person who had been responsible for these things had
suddenly abandoned their role. There had been a nurse
here, Fiona was sure of it—and not so long ago
either . . .

'Well, Miss Shore, here we are again.'

Once more the Mercedes slid noiselessly up the snowy
driveway to her hotel, and Fiona's only thought was the
likelihood of seeing him again before too long.

'Thank you,' she said quickly. 'I enjoyed today very
much, and although one never wishes for ill patients, at
least I saw how busy you can be this afternoon.'

'Yes, indeed.'

The doctor looked quietly at her for a moment or so
while she searched for her key, and then put a restraining hand on her shoulder.

'I have to go to Geneva tomorrow and will be away, I
think, for the remainder of your stay in Wengen. You
leave next Friday?'

'Saturday,' Fiona corrected him miserably, 'in the
morning.'

'Then I shall say *au revoir*, and take care of that ankle for the rest of your time here. Good luck in your career.'

'Goodbye,' Fiona murmured as he removed his hand from her shoulder and turned to get back into his car.

So that was that. Fiona almost ran up to her room, her feelings in chaos. She would never see him again. That was the reality. And yet what had she expected? He had shown her his clinic. He had given her a delicious lunch which she had ruined with her rude curiosity. He had thanked her for a small amount of help that she had been able to give him in the clinic and he had brought her to the hotel.

It was Saturday evening and now he had returned home after his busy day. He was looking forward to a quiet evening with his wife, perhaps to a small dinner party . . . Fiona could not bear to go on with the train of thought.

Sometime towards the morning, Fiona made up her mind that she would begin her holiday afresh tomorrow. She decided that she would rest her ankle. She had no more heart for skiing. Instead, she would explore the valley and the mountains using her ski pass to get her about with the lifts and telecabins. At last, she slept.

'The minute he thinks you're capable of getting down a mountain by yourself, he's off to explore fresh fields and pastures new,' Janice grimaced. She leaned her back against the wall of the ticket office. 'Honestly, he's a real Don Juan, but I've learned my lesson from him. I'll never trust *his* type again.'

She looked down ruefully at her stiff, bandaged leg, and then up at Fiona. Fiona smiled back at her new friend. They had met at Wengen station that morning and Fiona had been amazed to see the change in her patient of Saturday. She was easily recognisable as the bouncing, optimistic girl of the encounter in the ski shop. They had quickly exchanged names and decided to spend the day together.

'Erich Don Juan! That's about it. Shame about the mixed nationalities—but it's an international condition, it seems,' Fiona grinned.

'You reckon?' Janice scanned Fiona's face for more information.

'No, I know!' Fiona said with feeling and with no intention of elaborating upon her remark.

'My God!' exclaimed Janice. 'I'm not getting on *that*!'

The carriages of the funicular railway train looked as if they had been built to defy gravity and the effect was alarming. Nevertheless, it was too late to decide against travelling up to Mürren on it now. They got nervously in.

The train began its clunking crawl up the mountainside like a huge iron caterpillar journeying up the sheer face of a tree trunk, and the two girls tried to concentrate on the panoramic views out of the windows and to avoid looking back down the track.

Reaching the sunlit village of Mürren, they explored for as long as their injured legs allowed, absorbing the uncommercialised atmosphere of the farming village which seemed to have survived the skiers.

'What are you going to do about him?' Janice asked Fiona over lunch.

'Erich?'

'Yes.'

'Nothing,' Fiona stated. 'Tell him I don't want any more lessons.'

'He won't take no for an answer. Not from you,' Janice said, somewhat ruefully.

'Oh yes he will. He has before,' Fiona declared.

'Really?' the other girl replied, even more wistfully. She could not understand anybody refusing Erich anything.

'Poor Janice! He's no good, and you know it,' Fiona

said. 'It's worth waiting for somebody else to come along.'

Looking at her friend's dubious expression, Fiona wished she could accept her own counsel. The trouble was that she had been quite unable to forget Dr Eckhart, or to convince herself that somebody else would come along . . .

'How long are you here for, Janice?'

She suddenly decided that more intensive sight-seeing was the only answer to her obsessive state of mind and that, in Janice, she had the perfect companion.

They sealed their agreement to spend the rest of their holiday together with a clink of their *Glühwein* glasses.

'Disgusting, all this drinking at lunch-time,' Janice chastised herself happily. 'Still, one has to do something about that train journey down . . . Uggh!' She finished her mulled wine in a single gulp.

'How about another one?' Fiona suggested.

'Excellent idea,' Janice agreed, and ordered two more steaming aromatic drinks from the waitress.

Fiona folded her black silk dress and placed it carefully in her suitcase. She balanced the load with a tee-shirt. Well, she thought, I was right to wonder why I'd packed the silk dress. Her dinner date with Erich came back to her, swiftly followed by a re-run of the scene outside the night-club.

Her heart turned over. She had almost got to the end of her holiday without thinking about the finality of her departure from Wengen and her separation from Dr Eckhart. Now the full force of it came home to her.

She could hardly bear to think about leaving these mountains which she had got to know so well over the past few days. She had almost come to feel that she belonged here, high in the Bernese Oberland, far from the grey streets of Elchester.

She thought over her last conversation with Janice, who had turned out to be a physiotherapist in a London hospital. She had promised to do something positive about applying for a job in London, near her new friend if, when she got back to Elchester, she still felt she was in a rut. And now she knew that she would feel like that.

Yes. She would apply for jobs the moment she got back. Working with Daniel and the staff nurse would only be bearable if she knew that she was working her notice . . .

There was a light tap on her door.

'*Bitte*. Miss Shore, *ein Gast* . . .'

Fiona stared uncomprehendingly at her landlady. A guest? Who could be visiting her at this hour now that Janice had gone? Surely not Erich? Although she no longer felt anything but vague pity for the ski instructor, he was the last person whom Fiona wanted to see as she was mentally adjusting herself to going home.

'For me?' she said dully.

'*Ja*, Fräulein,' insisted the landlady, with just a hint of humour in her eyes.

Fiona followed her downstairs.

The elegant figure of Dr Eckhart stood quietly in the hall. He appeared to be examining a small framed water-colour of the hotel, and as he did so, he smoked his pipe.

Fiona stopped, frozen, on the last stair. Her heart felt as if it would rise up into her throat and choke her. She wished she had at least combed her hair. The doctor turned round and faced her calmly.

'Ah, Miss Shore. I am so sorry to intrude upon you so late in the evening, but I was afraid that I might miss you in the morning. I was uncertain as to your time of departure.'

'Oh, that's quite all right . . .' Fiona began, descending into the hall and then standing there, at a loss to know why he had come to see her.

'May we sit down?' he asked.

Fiona inwardly cursed her own thoughtlessness while the landlady showed them into the cosy dining-room. They sat down in front of the embers of the fire while Fiona wondered what the doctor was doing back from Geneva.

'I shall not keep you long,' he announced, 'but I should like you to consider carefully a request I have.'

Fiona held her breath while she waited for him to go on. She could not imagine what he could want of her.

'I should like you to consider delaying your departure from Switzerland and taking up the post of Sister-in-Charge of the Weiss Kreuz Klinik,' he said, delivering his words slowly and clearly so that Fiona could be left in no doubt as to his offer.

She stared at him in stunned silence.

'But—I had no idea . . .' she stammered.

'Of course,' he went on briskly, 'I understand that it is a big decision. A very big decision. Do you think you will be able to give me some idea of your feelings by early tomorrow morning?'

'Yes. Of course . . .' Fiona faltered.

'Then I shall not delay you further tonight,' the doctor said. 'I am sure you will want peace and solitude to think over my suggestion.'

He stood up, adjusted his coat collar and extended his right hand to Fiona. She shook hands with him numbly.

'Sleep well,' he told her, with a ghost of a smile.

That, thought Fiona as she watched him being shown out, is the very last thing that I shall do. But he had looked as if he knew that.

I should like you to consider delaying your departure . . .

He had said it exactly as if he were asking her to miss one train to share a cup of coffee with him, rather than give up her entire way of life and begin a new one.

Stunned, Fiona sat on her bed, the half-packed suitcase still open beside her. The doctor had been in the hotel for barely ten minutes, during which space of time he had succeeded in turning her world upsidedown.

Sister-in-Charge of the Weiss Kreuz Klinik.

Fiona stared out of the window at the dark-faced mountains which had offered her their welcome and support upon her arrival here two weeks before. But now they seemed to be hiding from her, rejecting responsibility for helping her to make the huge decision before her.

She recalled with a pang the preoccupation with Daniel Davenport which had poisoned her first days here, and she forced herself to face for the first time the reality of her return to work at St Helen's.

Daniel and Staff Nurse Kelly Morgan would have been working together almost every day for fourteen days. The new staff nurse would be familiar with the theatre by now, and would have made her mark upon the place in Fiona's absence. The realisations made Fiona's throat contract painfully.

How could she go back to all that? She got to her feet and crossed the room. And suddenly the mountains spoke to her of the surgeon whose life had touched her own so strangely. He too was cold and calm—and oddly reassuring. She could not pass up the chance to get to know him better, even if to do so meant that she had to struggle to come to terms with his separate private life and settle for a purely professional association with him.

Perhaps, in time, she would grow used to his coolness towards her and would learn to live comfortably with the knowledge of his idyllic personal life away from the clinic. It would be difficult for her, she knew.

But anything would be easier than being a helpless onlooker while Daniel and Staff Nurse Kelly played out their lives in front of her, exchanging their hidden smiles during working hours in General Theatre One at St Helen's Hospital. Fiona stood motionlessly confirming herself in her decision—and then she began to unpack.

Early tomorrow morning she would tell Dr Eckhart that she accepted his offer, and she would write a letter of resignation to the district health authority at home, even though breaking her contract with them would mean that she was unlikely to find a job with them again and would jeopardise her chances with other authorities.

Fiona Shore, burning her boats behind her and beginning a new life—she was beginning to feel quite like her old self again! She regretted only that Janice had gone home and there was nobody with whom she could toast her decision. For suddenly she had something definitely worth celebrating!

CHAPTER FIVE

THERE was still time to change her mind. Fiona approached the turning off the main street which led to the Weiss Kreuz Klinik with her heart in her mouth. It was a sparkling Alpine morning and everything about Wengen seemed to be conspiring against the guilty sense of duty to St Helen's Hospital with which she had awoken this morning. How could she think of leaving these pretty streets and the clean, clear air of the Bernese Oberland?

It was still two hours until her train left. Fiona knew that she had been offered the opportunity of a lifetime . . . yet what if Daniel's romance had ended? She had been happy at St Helen's but now, in the moment of acting upon her decision, it seemed that she had been *extremely* happy there.

She turned the corner and there ahead of her flew the White Cross. Beneath it lay a wealth of new experience for her. She had done no orthopaedic work since a brief spell during her training, and now she had a chance to learn new skills in this area of nursing care. The challenge of working in a new language and with people of many nationalities suddenly inspired Fiona with excited enthusiasm.

She would not even have to give up her beloved theatre work; here she would have another small theatre under her sole administration. She entered the reception area of the clinic confidently.

'Ah, Miss Shore. Good morning!'

The doctor greeted her formally, without noticeable anxiety to hear the decision she had arrived at. Fiona returned his greeting and said hello briefly to Renata, who was already in her place behind the reception desk.

'Come this way, Miss Shore.'

Dr Eckhart ushered Fiona into his consulting room, still betraying no sign of hurry or over-enthusiasm. Fiona followed him quietly and remained standing while he sat down behind his desk.

'I've decided to take up your kind offer,' she began, before he had time to speak. 'I shall stay on here as clinic sister.' She had been overwhelmed by a desire to speak while her mind was firmly made up.

'Excellent! I am delighted. You may start on Monday.' The doctor got to his feet and came towards Fiona with his right hand once more ready to take her own, and in his eyes and on his lips the first real smile that he had ever bestowed upon her. Fiona felt as if the moment had been worth the hours of agonised deliberating over her decision. And even as she stored it away in her memory, Dr Eckhart resumed his usual cool, aloof manner and gestured to her to follow him out of the consulting room.

'Renata, Miss Shore would like to see the document which I asked you to prepare.'

The receptionist gave Fiona a warm smile which indicated that she understood the significance of this request. She handed Fiona a two-page draft contract of employment in English, the first thing about which Fiona noticed was the huge sum in Swiss francs which was to be her monthly salary. She could barely stifle the gasp that rose to her lips.

'You are displeased?' Dr Eckhart said, a trace of annoyance or uncertainty in his voice. 'I took the liberty of drafting an agreement between us in the hope that you would indeed accept my offer . . .'

'Oh, no!' Fiona responded, looking up at him with frank eyes. 'I am delighted. I hope I shall fulfil your faith in my professional ability.'

'I have no doubt of that,' the doctor replied briskly, his voice once again fully confident. 'Be kind enough to read through the document and sign it this morning if you feel able to do so.' He gestured towards the table where a fresh pot of coffee stood awaiting her. 'And Renata, kindly show Miss Shore the apartment.'

The apartment? Fiona gazed from the door to the receptionist and back again to Dr Eckhart. A small smile played about his lips, as it had last night, at the sight of her astonished face.

'There is a modest flat available for the use of the Sister-in-Charge of the Weiss Kreuz Klinik. It is situated above the clinic here. I hope that it will be to your liking.'

Fiona once again had the disconcerting feeling of being in a dream. She rustled the paper of the contract softly between her fingers to put herself back in touch with reality. Taking a seat, she read through the terms of her new employment, then signed the paper slowly and carefully, giving it the gravity that she felt the act deserved.

The doctor had disappeared into his room and it was still early. Fiona looked about her at the elegant clinic and tried to realise the fact that this was her new domain.

'When you are ready, Miss Shore, I can show you the apartment,' Renata offered. She had slipped a bright red coat on over her blouse and skirt, and Fiona realised that she had not even taken her coat off yet this morning.

'Please call me Fiona,' she replied. 'I would love to see the flat.'

She was led out through the main doors of the clinic and round to the back of the building where a short flight of steps led up to a pretty wooden front door. Renata opened this and then handed the key to Fiona with a shy smile.

A stone-flagged hallway accommodated a coat stand and a rack for skis and boots. In typical Swiss style, it was big enough to change out of outdoor clothing in comfort before entering the living quarters—a necessity in a country where for much of the year snow and ice covered the earth.

The main area of the flat was reached through a second door, and Fiona found herself in a cosy, modern room. The walls had been painted in magnolia and there was a soft rose-coloured carpet on the floor. Velvet curtains in a darker rose hung from floor to ceiling at the french windows along one side of the room. A small dining table stood in one corner. There were two comfortable chairs upholstered in rose velvet, a glass coffee table and a television set. Overhanging wooden eaves protected the sunny balcony outside the french windows from snow, and a couple of deck-chairs stood out there.

Renata showed her the small modern bathroom, complete with bath and shower, and then the kitchen, which was well-equipped with a double stainless steel sink unit and a washing machine. The two bedrooms were perfect; a double room decorated in shades of blue, and a small guest room painted simply in white.

Excitement began to bubble up inside Fiona as her life here began to take shape in her imagination. She could already see her friends Claire and David coming here to stay with her for a holiday; imagine herself cooking in the kitchen and bathing comfortably after a day out on the slopes. She turned happily to Renata.

'It's lovely,' she exclaimed. 'I'm going to be so happy here!'

'Yes. The sister's apartment is indeed cosy. I hope that you will be so happy here.'

'I may move in straight away?'

'*Natürlich*: of course.' Renata looked as pleased as

Fiona felt about the prospect of her settling in here. The two girls went out and down the steps together side by side.

It was not until she was back in her hotel room collecting her things together and packing once again that it struck Fiona as odd that the sister's flat had seemed so clean and unused. She felt certain that it had never been lived in. And yet why should there be accommodation set aside for a nurse who had never existed? It seemed more and more mysterious, this silence surrounding her predecessor—for she was more certain now than ever before that there had been one.

Fiona smiled wryly at herself in the wardrobe mirror, dressed as she was in dark blue cords and a shirt for her first day in her new job. But it could not be helped. Until she got her first pay packet, her meagre and inappropriate wardrobe would have to suffice.

On the dot of eight o'clock, Renata met her in the clinic reception area.

'The apartment is comfortable?' she asked.

'Lovely, thank you, Renata,' Fiona replied. She took the flat package that Renata handed to her and unwrapped three new white dresses.

'I told your size in the shop the same as my own,' Renata explained shyly.

'You flattered me!' Fiona smiled. But the dresses fitted perfectly and Fiona felt fresh and confident by the time Dr Eckhart appeared fifteen minutes later.

He seemed to be in less than his normally calm frame of mind and it flashed through Fiona's head that this was the second time she had seen him obviously ruffled on his arrival at the clinic straight from his home. But she soon had reason to forget such things.

'Good morning, Sister,' he said with a brief nod of his head.

Fiona could not help her nervous smile. This new state of affairs between them was going to take some getting used to on her part, even if he found it perfectly natural, she reflected.

'Where do I begin?' she asked, trying to remain unmoved by his calm appraisal of her appearance. She thought that he approved of what he saw, but it was difficult to know this morning.

'As you will,' he replied, shrugging indifferently. 'There are no patients yet.'

He disappeared into his room and closed the door behind him.

So, this is the shape of things to come, thought Fiona! Well, if the doctor was looking for a demonstration of her initiative, then she would give him one.

She began by defrosting all three small fridges in the clinical area, then tidying them and replacing medical supplies. She went carefully and methodically through each of the medicine cupboards in the treatment rooms, noting expiry dates on tubes of ointment, packs of phials and bottles of tablets and discarding those that were out of date.

In one of the cupboards she found a memorandum with a section in English which explained Swiss drug control regulations, and she studied these until she had memorised them. Acquiring a new medicine order book from Renata, she began documenting all the drugs and noting quantities of dangerous drugs in stock, preparing to re-order supplies according to those she had removed from the shelves for some reason.

This done, she repeated the procedure with the supplies cupboards, making a bi-lingual list of everything to help herself learn the German names of things as she went along. She found items which again were past their 'use by' date, and these she discarded and re-ordered.

She attacked her new work with vigour and enthusi-

asm and coped easily with the three minor injuries which
turned up to interrupt her reorganisation session during
the morning. Dr Wilhelm gazed at her several times as
he went about his work, with apparent astonishment at
her energy. Twice, he grinned encouragingly at her.
Fiona felt happy and confident.

After a lunch-break during which she cemented her
friendship with Renata and convinced herself that the
receptionist was delighted to have another girl working
beside her in the clinic, Fiona continued with her work.
She saw hardly anything of Dr Eckhart all day and
guessed that he must have left the clinic on some business or other.

'Ah, Sister Shore. I would like a word with you.'

It was late afternoon and Fiona looked up, surprised,
from the cupboard which she was finishing tidying and
into the flinty eyes of her new employer. His voice
matched his look.

'Certainly,' she said pleasantly, smiling fleetingly at
him.

The doctor discreetly closed the door of the treatment
room and Fiona's confidence fled. What on earth was he
going to say to her that he did not want Renata to hear?

'You have been busy today.'

Fiona felt a flood of relief, in spite of the evident
displeasure in Dr Eckhart's voice. She was confident of
what she had done today, if nothing else.

'Yes. I've been taking stock and learning where things
are . . .' Fiona began.

'So I see,' the doctor replied ominously.

Fiona looked at him with mounting anxiety, but
waited patiently for him to continue with what he was
saying.

'And what are the objects in the two baskets at the
reception desk?' he enquired in icy tones.

'Oh, they are medicines and so on that are past their

expiry date. I'm going to re-order from the pharmacy according to the returns.'

'And you have moved things in the refrigerators,' he stated.

'Yes. I felt that things could be better organised in them, and I've put all the insulin in one place, together with the insulin syringes.' If these things were all that he was worried about, Fiona felt sure that the changes she had made were for the better. 'The plaster rooms have been rearranged too, slightly, so that we don't have to walk far with the wet bandages . . .'

'Miss Shore,' the doctor interrupted her in a furious voice, 'I do not wish you to reorganise the clinic around me. I did not employ you to do so and I would be grateful if you confined yourself in future to nursing patients.'

Fiona stared at her employer. His face was flushed and his eyes dark with anger. She recognised real fury compared with the superficial irritation that he had displayed during her very first encounter with him on the train. She could not imagine what she had done to deserve this onslaught. He had left her to her own devices and she had spent her first day under his employment fruitfully and independently. How on earth had she offended him?

'But . . .' she began.

'You may go off duty now,' he interrupted her furiously.

The words amounted to a dismissal. He was ordering her out of his sight! Fiona turned and left the room, her eyes blinded with the tears that she had been fighting so hard to control. She rushed past the reception desk, hardly hearing Renata's cheerful, '*Auf Wiedersehen!*'

Once in her flat, Fiona allowed the tears to flow. She sat down in her sitting-room and sobbed unreservedly. What had she done wrong? What had provoked his attack upon her? She was as deeply hurt by the personal insult as by the professional one. After all, she had spent half her working life coping with rude surgeons—but this was different. It had been almost as if it was her actual presence that he had found intolerable.

Suddenly, the enormity of her decision to stay in Switzerland hit Fiona. She had posted the letter of resignation to her employing authority in England and there was no going back on that. It was too late for this awful fear of the future that she now felt. Yet if the doctor was going to turn out to be an irrational tyrant . . . Had the charm that she had glimpsed in him been put on simply to trap her here . . . yet why?

She controlled her tears and went into the kitchen. She put the kettle on, the physical act soothing her nerves. She had managed so successfully to put Elchester out of her mind. Surely homesickness was not going to hit her now, just as she settled into her new job?

There was a gentle knocking at the outer door of her flat and then, just as she thought she must have imagined it, the unfamiliar ringing of her own doorbell. Fiona answered it to find Renata shyly on her doorstep.

'Come in!' she said. She had never been so pleased to see anybody in her whole life. 'I am making tea,' she said. 'English tea!'

'Wonderful!' said the receptionist, placing the folded clothes that Fiona had been wearing that morning on a kitchen chair. 'All is good?'

Fiona knew that Renata knew that she had been crying. She carried the tea through on a tray and placed it on the coffee table, and the two girls sat down.

'I'm just tired,' Fiona said, pouring tea. 'Too much excitement all in one day. New job, new life, new everything . . .'

But her new friend was not to be so easily fooled.

'The doctor was angry with you?' she asked, her frank grey eyes holding Fiona's dark, troubled turquoise gaze.

'Yes,' Fiona admitted with a sigh, 'he was. And I really don't know why.'

'I saw what you did today. Everything was so beautifully tidy and clean when you were finished . . .' Renata gently commented.

'Then why was he so cross?' Fiona burst out, unable to control herself any longer.

'Perhaps you make too many changes,' Renata suggested carefully. 'Perhaps he liked better the way things were.'

'But the fridges were dirty,' Fiona objected, 'and some of the medicines were out of date. That is dangerous.'

'It is also dangerous to do things too quickly for Dr Eckhart. Some things are . . . not allowed to be changed.'

The receptionist's voice was soft, but Fiona detected a distinct warning in her words.

'Why not?' Fiona ventured outright. Nobody was going to help her to understand this man if Renata was not.

'Because . . .' Renata began, and then seemed to think better of her answer. 'Because of some personal reason,' she corrected herself.

'Personal to Dr Eckhart?' Fiona persisted, but she knew that it was no good, and that even Renata was not going to be drawn further on this subject.

'Perhaps, yes . . .'

'Well, now I know,' Fiona said with irony, but anxious to release her new-found friend from cross-examination. 'One lives and one learns.'

Renata looked at her, puzzled.

'An old English saying,' said Fiona, grinning. 'More tea?'

Renata's relief was obvious and touching. Fiona resolved not to test her loyalty again, but to cope as best she could with her new circumstances alone. She poured more tea for them both. She felt better and began to enjoy the company of her very first guest.

If Fiona had expected or hoped for an apology from her employer for his outburst she would have been disappointed. But apart from this episode, she felt that her first fortnight as Sister-in-Charge of the Weiss Kreuz Klinik had gone well.

Dr Eckhart had adopted a distant air with her which Fiona had grown to recognise and respect. She secretly regretted the passing of the familiarity between them which had begun to develop by the end of their first Saturday when she had toured the clinic—but that was all behind them now, and it was no good wishing that things were different between herself and her employer.

Fiona thought along these lines while she pushed open the door to the little operating theatre and went inside. She looked quickly around the silent, spotless room and up at the wall clock. She would damp-dust and lay up emergency trays as usual in case there was a case.

Working, she wondered with surprise why they were so quiet this morning. She had already got used to expecting frantic Saturdays at the clinic as weekend skiers from Bern and even further afield descended upon Wengen. Fiona smiled to herself at the thought that she was soon to join them. Now that her ankle was completely better, she had been seriously considering spending her next days off on the *pistes*.

'Ah, Sister, here you are!'

Fiona spun round from the autoclave which she was in the process of filling with trays of instruments. Dr Eckhart ran an expert eye over the trays.

'We're going to need all those, plus pins and plates,' he informed Fiona. 'The case is on its way to us now. Internal reduction and fixation of a fractured femur—

with wide separation of the bone fragments.'

The moment that he had gone, Fiona flew into action. The patient would be in theatre within the next half-hour. She closed the door of the autoclave and began sterilising the instruments while she thought methodically through the coming operation so that she would be able to anticipate all the surgeon's needs.

The most important nursing responsibility in a case of this sort was, Fiona remembered, the cleansing of the skin over the site of the fracture. Any introduction of infection could lead to infection of the bone itself—osteomyelitis, which was almost impossible to cure and could cripple the patient. So the wound must be kept scrupulously clean.

Fiona set up a tray for shaving the patient over the operation site, and then another with Betadine lotion for scrubbing the shaved skin. The addition of an antiseptic ointment completed her skin prep tray.

This was the first time that Fiona had scrubbed up for her new boss. Dr Wilhelm had always been on hand to do so up until now, and Fiona had been spared the ordeal. Now it was upon her suddenly, and the case would be a complicated one. Fiona felt extremely nervous, laying out packs of sterile gowns for them both and guessing at Dr Eckhart's glove size in order to lay out two pairs for him. She surprised herself by remembering that some orthopaedic surgeons used two pairs of gloves as a safeguard against glove puncture from sharp bone ends.

Showering quickly so as to leave the room free for the surgeon, Fiona mentally ran through her preparations. She wrapped herself in a towel and stepped into the changing room. Opening a cupboard, she wondered whether she would find any theatre gear to fit her; these were among the few cupboards that she had not yet explored and tidied.

It was a pleasant surprise to find a neat stack of small blue female pyjamas on one of the shelves. She put a pair on and they fitted nicely. Grabbing a mask and a pair of overshoes, Fiona was about to take a paper cap to cover her hair when she noticed a small pile of neatly folded muslin squares behind the box. She was amazed to find her preferred method of keeping her hair tidy here, just as if she had been in her own theatre at home!

She took a white square and twisted her hair up inside, tying it into a turban. If the doctor had really not employed a nurse, then all that Fiona could imagine was that he had had a female medical assistant . . .

'Take that off!' The order rang around the little changing room, making Fiona jump. Dr Eckhart was glaring through at her from the other side of the shower-room, an expression of pained anger on his face.

'What?' Fiona asked, dismayed by his command and obvious fury.

'That . . . *head-dress*,' he hissed the word at her.

Fiona reached up guiltily and quickly unwound the turban. Her hair fell down around her face, covering her confusion. The doctor watched for a moment and then stormed out of the room and her sight. Fiona tucked her hair up under a paper cap and miserably discarded the muslin square into a laundry bag. Was she never going to manage to do anything to please this man, she wondered? Suddenly, the thought of standing next to a sullen, imperious Dr Eckhart for the next couple of hours looked most unappealing to Fiona.

It was a relief to recognise the anaesthetist as the same man who had been called to the clinic the day of Janice and Sue's accident and, sure enough, he smiled and waved as he induced the patient on the other side of the operating room from where Fiona had begun to scrub up. When she began her skin preparations the anaesthetist soothed her nerves with his cheerful congratulations over her new appointment and stories about how he had worked in Liverpool as a houseman during the war.

She half listened to his pleasant banter while concentrating the majority of her attention upon the job in hand and the operation as it would progress from here. She made up her mind that however rude Dr Eckhart might take it into his head to be to her, and however hurt she was by his rudeness, she would demonstrate to him how competent she was as a theatre sister. No matter what!

She could not possibly have been prepared for the almost instinctive ease with which she found she could work with this surgeon. They reduced the fracture, bringing the bone-ends into their correct alignment for healing, and fixing them in that position with pins and plates. Fiona paid rapt attention to the procedure and found that she could anticipate almost all of Dr Eckhart's needs. Meanwhile, she marvelled at the skill in the strong, sensitive fingers that worked beside her own.

Dr Wilhelm appeared to 'run' for Fiona about half-way through the operation, and she was glad of his help in choosing from the packs of stitches and selection of drains that she had laid out, uncertain of what exactly the surgeon would want.

It was not until he was closing the skin with a line of neat, uninterrupted silk sutures that Dr Eckhart spoke.

'I'll put a couple of clips in around the drain,' he told Fiona, and she was surprised by the conciliatory tone of his voice. She handed him clips and an introducer. 'Thank you, Sister.'

Fiona glanced at the eyes above the mask. Returned to their task, they were hidden by lowered, dark lashes. She looked at the faint crow's feet at the corner of his lids. For whom did he laugh, this cold, serious man? She had seen him laugh with his children. Did he laugh with his wife, too? Suddenly, Fiona was overwhelmed by a desire to break through his reserve and for him to smile at her again.

The surgeon finished closing the skin and turned away from his patient, peeling off his gloves as he did so. He shrugged his shoulders slowly and sensually, stretching his back muscles in sudden release from the tension of the operation.

Fiona remained at the place where she had stood for two hours. With the patient gone, wheeled into the recovery area by the anaesthetist, Dr Wilhelm returned to another case and Dr Eckhart gone from her side, she felt strangely exposed and alone in the middle of the operating room. She was surrounded with the debris of the procedure that had just taken place, and filled with the void that the tension of operating had left in her.

She began checking all the instruments on her Mayo tables and sorting them into disposable and non-disposable items. For a long time she sorted, counted and checked. Then she wearily turned away from the order she had created, peeled off her own gloves and decided that she would finish clearing away after she had had a cup of coffee. Her head felt light and her feet numb. She had missed lunch.

It was hours later, at almost five o'clock, that Dr Eckhart strode silently into the little operating room again. Fiona had just finished and the place was immaculate again. She was exhausted, more with emotional than physical tiredness, and was thinking about an evening in front of the television in her little flat.

'Oh, you surprised me!' Fiona exclaimed. She had been working alone for so long that it was disconcerting to feel another presence beside her.

'I am surprised myself to find you still here.'

'I have only just finished clearing up,' she explained.

'You will make yourself indispensable,' the surgeon said with a slow smile.

Fiona tried to cope with the effect that this had upon her.

'Nobody is ever indispensable,' she managed to say in a light voice.

'I don't know that that is always the case,' the surgeon replied.

He was standing very close to Fiona. She found herself neither able to move out of his disturbing presence, nor to respond appropriately to his remark.

She was almost unable to believe the messages that were moving through her body when she felt his firm hands upon her shoulders. She looked up into his face and registered with a thrill the softness in his eyes. An age seemed to pass, and Fiona closed her eyes for an instant, during which time she felt his warm mouth brush her own.

Then, as if he had instantly thought better of his act, Dr Eckhart moved away, leaving Fiona standing alone again, staring at her employer. She knew her eyes told him of her response to his kiss.

'Thank you for your expert assistance today,' he said quietly. 'Isn't it time you went off duty now?'

'Yes,' Fiona answered hastily, 'yes, it is. I'm going now.'

She felt vaguely surprised that her legs obeyed her and took her out of his presence. She made her way swiftly through the clinic, nodding goodbye to Renata and Dr Wilhelm as she passed the reception desk. The last time she had rushed from the clinic like this it had been in response to quite different behaviour on Dr Eckhart's part . . . She did not know what to think.

Fiona stooped and picked up the letter from the door-mat. She noted the Elchester postmark, but was in too much of a confused state to seriously wonder who had written to her so soon. Her heart and mind were still in the operating room; his kiss still fluttered on her lips and she could feel the warmth of his breath on her cheek, the vigour of his presence and the insistence of his hold.

What could have prompted such an act on his part? There had certainly never been any indication that such a thing could possibly happen between them.

The only explanation was a simple, straightforward one, she decided. He had been pleased with the way that the day had gone and pleasantly surprised by her ability as a theatre nurse. He had felt an impulsive urge to kiss her and had done so—and he was now probably regretting it at his leisure. Fiona tried to accept the idea that she had been kissed by the surgeon in a meaningless expression of his own satisfaction, while she was left with her ache for him cruelly enhanced. She would never be able to eradicate that moment from her memory; never be able to forget that instant which had stolen so suddenly upon her that she had almost failed to taste it. He would resume his cold, dispassionate, remote attitude towards her, and she would hardly be able to get through the next day off duty before she could see him again.

Almost without thinking, Fiona opened the envelope which had sat forgotten in her lap for the past ten minutes. She took out the letter, unfolded it and read the contents.

Dear Fiona,
I know you will be surprised to hear from me. I had hoped and expected to be able to talk to you in person and was very upset to learn that you had resigned from your post here and were staying on in Switzerland. Why?

Fiona, I must see you. It is all over now between Kelly and myself and I deeply regret hurting you. I know that I have no right to ask your forgiveness—but I do. You must know how much you always meant to me. I have missed you greatly.

Is it really too late for us? I know that we can be happy together again. I have applied for a consultancy in Bristol and expect to get it. Please say that you will share my future with me.

I hope to hear from you soon,
Daniel.

Fiona gasped out loud.

Daniel! The name jumped off the page at her. It was loaded with associations and charged with conflicting emotions. Daniel writing to her and asking for her forgiveness! It was more than she had ever dared to hope for.

She read the letter again, and then once more, trying to imagine how he had felt and looked as he had written it. From the typed envelope it was obvious that he had given it to his secretary to post. Fiona smiled. Typical of Daniel not to bother even to send a love letter himself! But in spite of her smile, Fiona sensed insincerity between the lines for which she had once so longed.

Yet she still wanted to believe him. She wanted to trust him again. She had loved him so much and hoped for so much with him. Even if he were to betray her again . . . perhaps . . . The thought of the tenderness in his eyes over that long summer together, and the memory of his kisses, swept over Fiona.

But, to her surprise, the thought of them brought back to her a much more recent kiss which stubbornly remained in her mind, blotting out memories of Daniel.

It was no good. She had changed her life and no matter what confusion, what difficulties and what troubles the new one brought her, she could not go back to the old, even if Daniel really loved her . . .

Now the thought of his treachery was stronger than any hope for happiness with him. She crumpled up the letter in her hand and threw it into the waste-paper basket.

CHAPTER SIX

FIONA had succeeded in banishing Daniel's letter from her mind. She had spent the whole of Wednesday on the ski slopes, thoroughly enjoying her day off and picking up her skiing where she had been forced to abandon her new skills. Once she had caught sight of Erich and he had waved cheerily to her. It was nice to be free.

She had resolved to make the most of the slopes from now on. In a couple of months the snow would begin to disappear, and so would the skiers and the sport. It would be the time for cow-scented meadows, warm sunshine and wild flowers. Fiona looked forward to her first Alpine spring.

'There, is that better?' she asked. The figure-of-eight bandage which she had just applied to her patient's shoulder to immobilise his fractured clavicle was neat and effective.

'Much,' he informed her gratefully. He was a lively Cockney with a very worried girlfriend waiting for him in reception.

Fiona explained that the pad of felt beneath his arm was there to protect the nerves and blood vessels there, but that if he got uncomfortable he should feel free to move his arm out from his body and rest it on the arm of a chair or on a table.

'You should try to use it as naturally as possible, in any case,' Fiona told him, 'to prevent getting a frozen shoulder.'

'Make a change from frozen feet, Sister!'

'Ho-ho!' Fiona responded drily. She had listened to a

stream of wit from her patient ever since he had presented himself.

'And you can take something for the pain now that we've finished with you.'

He gave her the thumbs up sign and rejoined his girlfriend after thanking her profusely. Fiona heard him announcing that he'd 'bust' his shoulder. It sounded impressive!

She had grown used to the pattern of her new working life. Now, tidying up after her last patient in preparation for the next, she thought how very pleasant and satisfying it was. She dealt with sprains and uncomplicated fractures with ease now, and had even discovered an unexploited talent in herself for taking and reading X-rays. Her diagnostic skills were positively encouraged by Dr Wilhelm with whom she worked for much of the time on minor injuries. While Fiona had been unprepared for this extension of her nursing role, she had found that it added greatly to her job satisfaction.

It was at the X-ray machine that Dr Eckhart found her a short time later. The patient, sent in soon after she had finished with her Cockney was, Fiona was almost sure, suffering from a simple sprained wrist. But she was X-raying to exclude the possibility of a Colles' fracture, a common injury sustained when skiers tried to break a fall with their outstretched arm.

'Keep as still as you possibly can,' Fiona asked the woman before retreating behind her lead shielding screen.

The machine buzzed and clicked. Fiona rearranged the patient's hand over a clean plate, withdrew and the machine buzzed and clicked again for a lateral view.

'That's fine. Thank you,' Fiona said. 'Would you mind waiting outside for a couple of minutes please?'

'A Colles'?' Dr Eckhart asked casually from the seat he had taken near the reporting desk.

'I'm pretty sure it's just sprained,' Fiona returned, 'but we'll see.'

She fervently hoped that Dr Eckhart would leave her alone before the X-ray plates were ready for viewing. She found being alone with him difficult enough to cope with sometimes, especially here in an empty room. The memory of his kiss, far from fading, had grown even stronger in her mind.

He did not go. Fiona nervously pushed the X-ray pictures up under the clips on the viewer and switched the lights on. There, clearly and unmistakably displayed, was the 'silver-fork deformity' typical of a Colles' fracture.

Fiona blushed and Dr Eckhart turned to face her, a half-smile on his lips. He pulled his pipe out of the pocket of his sports jacket and began slowly and deliberately to fill it with tobacco.

'Well,' he said, 'I'm glad you're not infallible *all* the time.'

Fiona looked for sarcasm or cynicism or both on his face but, finding neither, at last allowed herself to return his smile.

'I'm never left alone with such important decisions,' she explained. 'Dr Wilhelm always double-checks the X-ray pictures.'

'I'm sure that he does, Sister Shore,' Dr Eckhart said. He lit his pipe.

'I don't want you to think that I've been over-stepping the responsibility you've given me or abusing my freedom to develop my role here,' she said with quiet dignity. But her heart was racing. She feared his rages now. She had been hurt enough by the apparent indifference with which he had treated her ever since he had kissed her and she knew that if he shouted at her again she would not be able to help crying openly in front of him.

'I do not think anything of the sort, Sister,' he told her, smoking thoughtfully. Fiona turned her attention to taking the X-ray pictures down. There was an intensity in his quiet presence which she found almost unbearable.

'I must get the plaster room ready for the Colles',' she murmured.

'I will set it myself,' he told her. 'With your help, of course, Sister,' he added in slightly bantering tones.

Fiona nodded and swiftly left the X-ray room, taking the plates with her. She settled the patient in the plaster room and Dr Eckhart joined them there. They worked quickly and harmoniously to reduce and set the fracture, and the only words spoken during the procedure passed between Fiona and the patient as she explained each step before it happened.

'No,' Dr Eckhart began, 'I do not think you are misinterpreting your role here in the least.'

Fiona looked up with surprise from the white slurry of plaster-of-Paris which she was sluicing down the sink. He had resumed their conversation on an hour ago exactly as if it had never been interrupted.

'On the contrary, I am extremely pleased by the way in which you have fitted into and enhanced the running of the clinic.'

Fiona dried her hands carefully in order to maximise the time during which she could reasonably keep her back to her employer. At last she turned to face him, hoping that normal colour had returned to her face.

'I am glad that that is how you feel . . .' she began.

'I should have liked to have waited until your fourth week here proved that your efficiency was not a fluke,' he went on, and she felt her palms moisten, 'but unfortunately I shall not be here to witness the undoubtedly triumphant completion of your first month with us.'

Fiona let out the breath that she had been quietly

holding in order to control herself. A sick sense of forboding stole over her. This man had the ability to make her live through storms of emotions that left her limp.

'Where are you off to?' she enquired in what she hoped was a normal voice.

'Just another lecture tour,' he said. 'Geneva again.'

'Ah!' Fiona did not know how to continue this conversation.

'So I wondered whether you would do me the honour of dining with me before I leave?'

Once again, she saw the flecked green eyes dance with amusement at the confusion they found in her face. She had lost her voice.

'Well, Sister? Do you already have an engagement for Sunday evening?' he persisted, apparently enjoying himself at her expense.

'No. No, of course not,' Fiona managed to say at last. 'I would love to have dinner with you. I . . .'

'Then that's settled,' said the doctor. 'I'll pick you up at eight.'

He strode out of the plaster room and Fiona sat down hard upon the chair recently vacated by her patient. Dinner with Dr Eckhart was one of the dreams which she had strictly forbidden herself. Quickly, before her excitement could rise, she rationalised the invitation. He was genuinely pleased with her professional performance—and he was Swiss, with all the courtesy that his nationality had bred in him. This was what he had implied it to be; a formal thanks and one which he had obviously planned for the end of her first month if things went well. But still, Fiona could not suppress her pleasure, and she wondered how she was going to get through the three long days that stretched between now and Sunday evening.

*   *   *

Fiona pulled the soft black silk over her head and it fell about her in a familiar cool caress. She knew that the dress suited her. It was gently gathered on to a high, modest neckline, and from here fell in fine folds to the waist. A thin rope of jet beads secured the silk at the waist before it fell to just below the knee in a flattering, classic and undating length.

Tonight it felt exactly right. Fiona had searched the shops and had been unable to find anything that suited her better. The high black shoes which she had bought with part of her first pay cheque specially to go with the dress were simple, expensive and elegant. They complemented the dress perfectly.

She wore no jewellery, but had put on just enough of her favourite perfume over her pulse spots. Spraying on the *Rive Gauche*, Fiona had remembered for the first time in years her mother once telling her how to apply perfume so that it was released as the body got warmer. She had wondered then—when she was thirteen or so—when she would ever need so useless a piece of advice. It had been a long time before she had found a boy mature enough to interest her . . .

She looked in the mirror and nervously glanced at her watch. It was five to eight. The girl in the mirror had a soft mass of shining auburn hair, bright turquoise eyes and slightly flushed cheeks above the small mouth. Her skin was clear and lovely against the back silk, and her slim legs and simple shoes accentuated the dramatic line of her dress.

The doorbell rang and she felt her heart move in response. So much for mother's advice about the perfume, she thought. It'll be used up before I reach the front door at this rate!

He smiled down at her while she waited what seemed an interminable time for him to let her close the door behind them and follow him down the steps. She was glad for her white fur coat and gathered it around her as the snowy night air reached her bath-warm body.

In the car he asked after her last couple of days at work, during which he had not been around the clinic. He hoped that she was not too tired to enjoy the evening. She answered dreamily. She was aware only of the presence beside her and of the evening spreading out before her like a lifetime.

'Here we are.' Dr Eckhart brought the Mercedes softly to a halt in a small side-street. Fiona glimpsed a painted sign which read *Bistro Hofman Frère* and then was ushered into a tiny, cosy entrance hall where a young man in a dinner jacket gently took her coat.

While he was hanging it up, Dr Eckhart produced a tiny red rose bud which he handed to Fiona. He watched for a moment while she tried with trembling fingers to pin it on her dress, and then secured the rose for her in the neckline above her right breast.

'Thank you,' she breathed. He smiled at her.

'First, an aperitif.'

Fiona was led into a small bar which was separated from the dining area of the restaurant by a hand-painted wooden screen and a wall of flowering pot plants. It was difficult to decide exactly what gave this place its French provincial atmosphere, but that was what it had. The bar was intimate and the barman reserved. The couple sat down and the doctor ordered Pernod for himself and a gin with tonic for Fiona. The black silk dress fell softly about her as she sat on the high stool, her straight back the only external evidence of her inner tension.

'You look very lovely this evening, Miss Shore,' Dr Eckhart said.

'Thank you,' she again heard herself say. And then, 'Won't you call me Fiona?'

They sipped their drinks, and while they did so the doctor began to talk about a trip he had made last summer to the Caribbean. He described silver-white sands, glittering seas and the myriad jewel-like fish that he had seen. He had apparently been diving and wanted to return this year to take a more advanced course.

'It is a very romantic spot, Fiona—or would be, under different circumstances.'

He looked quizzically at her, half-teasing. She swallowed the last of her drink suddenly and with difficulty. So he was there on his own—or he did not find his wife's company romantic? Fiona's heart sank. She tried to put away the thought that the doctor was playing with her feelings and to concentrate upon taking this evening for what it was; a simple expression of his professional gratitude towards her.

'I am sure that it is . . . a romantic place, Dr Eckhart,' Fiona said in a quiet voice, 'if you are in that frame of mind.'

'Frames of mind, eh?' The doctor chuckled. 'My name is Hans, Fiona, and I think that it is time that you called me by my name.'

'Your table is ready, Dr Eckhart.'

Fiona looked up to find a woman of about forty standing beside them, her dark hair coiled at the nape of her neck and her large, dark eyes expressive. She was wearing a dark print dress, tight in the bodice and flowing in the skirt.

'Thank you, Alison,' Dr Eckhart responded warmly. 'You are as beautiful as ever this evening!'

The woman smiled, blushing slightly. They followed her graceful walk to a corner in the next room; a table crowned with mauve and white freesias and a candle in a silver holder. But Fiona was thinking about the compliment that she had received earlier, and the one that had just been paid to the woman. It was either merely courtesy, or so overused as to be meaningless . . .

'Alison is a very old friend. She is the widow of the

man who began the bistro here, who was French and died under tragic circumstances early last year. Luckily for us, Alison, who is English, decided to stay on and keep the restaurant—which is the best in Wengen, incidentally. She allows me to practice my English,' he smiled.

'I'm sure that you do not need to practise your English. It's excellent.'

Fiona thought about the look that Alison had given them both as she left them at their table. It had been a curious look, almost affectionate. Like the look that the woman who had run the place where he had taken her to lunch had given them. Fiona wondered how often the doctor ate out with women other than his wife.

'And you are getting most proficient with the German language. I am impressed with your progress,' the doctor said.

The head waiter arrived and checked that they had everything they needed, leaving them with menus and a wine list. It was clear that the waiter knew the doctor well and had been allocated responsibility for his well-being for the duration of the meal.

Fiona lost herself in the menu. It was not too big, and full of exquisite dishes. She struggled with her schoolgirl French, determined not to ask for guidance unless she had to do so.

Having decided upon what she would eat, Fiona looked up and watched the man sitting opposite her while he chose his meal. She looked at the fine dark curves of the eyebrows and the dark lashes against his cheeks, and observed the two deep lines that ran down towards the corners of the full, strong mouth. She was struck by a disturbing discrepancy between the mental image that she had built up for herself of this man and the reality of the resting face before her. There was, she forced herself to admit, nothing of the philanderer in those features. She knew that she instinctively trusted and respected this man.

'What will you have?' he asked.

'The *salade de crevettes* and then roast saddle of venison, I think,' she responded.

'A good choice. The game is always very good here. It is hunted locally.'

The wine waiter appeared and conferred with her companion in the same respectful way in which other members of staff had done. A bottle of chilled Muscadet was brought to their table and a little poured for the doctor to taste. More was poured for each of them, and the doctor lifted his glass and clinked it against Fiona's.

'To your long happy life in Wengen!' he smiled.

'I have enjoyed it so far,' Fiona responded modestly. The white wine was dry and fresh on her tongue. She sipped appreciatively.

'You have not been homesick?'

Fiona started. The question brought a flood of memories; grey streets, her little flat in Monmouth Gardens, daffodils and crocuses pushing up through the winter-brown earth of the park and walks to the hospital through Elchester's deserted early morning streets.

St Helen's and the operating theatre presented themselves to her mind's eye and then, before she could stop them, vivid visions of the cold, amused faces of Kelly Morgan and Daniel Davenport. Her heart lurched and she suddenly felt sick.

'Fiona?'

She looked up from the still depths of the wine into which she had been staring, and into Dr Eckhart's slightly worried face.

'The wine is delicious,' she said. But her mind was busy re-reading Daniel's letter. *I have missed you greatly* . . .

'You are thinking of England?' Dr Eckhart gently enquired.

At that moment the head waiter brought their first course, and Fiona was able to occupy herself with unfolding her napkin and laying it in her lap.

'This looks delicious!' she said brightly.

'*Bon appétit*,' said the waiter, and the doctor filled their glasses again.

Fiona lifted her fork automatically. She regretted having to touch the beautifully-presented dish in front of her. She tasted a prawn, bit into some apple and then into crisp celery hearts and walnuts. And all the time her enjoyment was impaired by the presence in her mind of Daniel Davenport.

Six weeks ago—even a month ago—she would have been overjoyed to get his letter and the chance of happiness that it offered her. Yet now she felt nothing but unease and distrust.

She looked once more at her companion. To her surprise, he had paused in his eating and was watching her face. She met his look. It was warm and frank and she felt that she might melt under it.

She told herself not to be so affected by him. If this, or rather *he*, was the reason behind her negative response to Daniel's plea for forgiveness, then she should find a better reason to reject her former lover. There was no use in her dreaming about anything other than a purely professional relationship with the man opposite her, for he was established, sophisticated, mature and married with three lovely children. If he was smiling gently at her now, it was because he saw her confusion and pitied her.

Meanwhile, their plates were removed and the wine waiter brought a bottle of rich red wine. The candle-light played across the features of the doctor while he discussed something with the wine waiter. There was nothing superior in his attitude towards the other man; they discussed the wine expert to expert, each listening to the other with obvious respect for his opinion.

Unobtrusively, while the wine waiter and Hans Eckhart were still talking, the roast venison arrived, magnificent upon an oval silver dish. Fiona watched, fascinated, while the head waiter served their portions of the dark, aromatic meat with tiny golden glazed onions, shining mushroom caps which had been sautéed in butter and triangular crisp *croutons*.

Fiona felt the warmth of the candle-light on her face as she inhaled the delicious smell of her main course and watched while two glasses were filled with ruby vintage Gevrey-Chambertin.

'I hope that this meets with your approval.'

'It is all absolutely perfect, Hans,' Fiona smiled.

She was surprised at how easily she had used his name for the first time, and their new intimacy seemed to break the spell that memories of Daniel had cast over her. She began to eat with enjoyment and he began a relaxed conversation about his young colleague, Dr Wilhelm. With dignity, and without gossip, the senior doctor made it clear that Dr Wilhelm and Renata had been involved together for some time and that Renata, who was apparently much sought after by local young men, had been unwilling to commit herself.

Fiona listened quietly while he talked and they ate. She knew a little about the feelings that Renata had for the serious young doctor, and even that the receptionist was on the point of agreeing to marry him, so she had to stifle her smile at the doctor's concluding remark to the effect that he wished they would marry and get it over with.

'But . . . I mean, that wouldn't make any difference to their working life in the clinic, would it?' Fiona asked innocently.

'No. Of course, I suppose not. But it is difficult to work together every day when things are . . . unresolved in one's personal life—is it not, Fiona?'

Fiona blushed deeply and her appetite fled. What on earth was he talking about? She lifted her napkin and hid her mouth briefly from his steady gaze, then took a sip of wine. He, without taking his eyes from her face, refilled her glass.

'Yes. I suppose . . . I mean, I should think . . .' Fiona began.

'So. The venison was good, was it not?' the doctor interrupted her mercifully.

She took the menu he offered her and tried to choose a third course while she ordered her thoughts. So he had guessed how she felt. She was obviously pretty transparent.

She ordered a tangerine ice and it arrived in a tiny natural dish of fruit skin, surrounded with a wreath of camellia leaves, tangerine slices and crystallised violets. She had never seen such a beautiful sight on a dinner table. The ice was home-made and exquisite.

Eating it, Fiona decided that she would keep a tighter control on her feelings from now on. She had committed herself to her new job at the Weiss Kreuz Klinik and she was enjoying it. If the price for her new life was this silent secret that was growing inside her, then she would simply have to pay it. She finished her sorbet and sat back.

The doctor ordered coffee and offered Fiona a liqueur, but she refused and sipped the mineral water that had been brought to her with her dessert. She watched her companion accept a brandy and a cigar with obvious pleasure.

'I hope you have no problems of any kind while I am away,' he said, leaning back comfortably in his chair and lighting his cigar. 'But I am confident that Dr Wilhelm

will be able to help you . . . and not only with reading
X-rays.' His eyes twinkled.

Fiona looked at the doctor, but this time without fear
for his expression or the meaning behind his words. A
week in Geneva. It was nothing to him, she realised with
a pang.

'He is always most kind and helpful with me,' Fiona
said of the medical assistant.

'And so he should be,' Dr Eckhart pronounced. 'I
have great faith in you both, and I hope he and Renata
can spare a little of their time to spend with you out of
working hours if you feel homesick . . .'

'Oh,' Fiona interrupted, 'Renata and I are good
friends already. I see quite a bit of her outside work.'

'Good. And then there is your skiing friend if you
need an evening out . . .'

Fiona looked sharply at the doctor and caught a hint of
sarcasm behind the smile. She did not know how to
answer him without letting him know just how completely and utterly he was wrong in his assumptions
about Erich and herself. Or how the thought of any
other man had been dismissed and replaced . . .

'I was never too much struck,' she said slowly, 'by my
ski instructor.'

It had sounded quite natural, even flippant. And she
had told the truth. It was up to him whether or not he
accepted her word. She watched the fine eyebrows lift
for a moment and a question flicker in the flecked eyes
before the calm self-containment returned to his face.

She wondered whether he really did know what the
next week would be like for her without his presence, his
voice about the clinic. She wondered whether he was
watching her from the wings, amused by the confusion
into which she was thrown by him. Her heart turned over
at the thought.

'More coffee, mademoiselle?' The silver coffee-pot

caught the candle-light and shone softly. Fiona helped herself to cream and the doctor smiled at her, accepted a second cup of coffee himself and stared into the amber depths of his brandy. Fiona tried not to believe that the evening would end.

Outside, the night sky was deep sapphire blue and dancing with stars. The moon shone among them all, apart, casting its soft light on the far mountain peaks and turning the road that wound away into them silver.

Fiona felt the light touch of the doctor's hand upon her arm, and he led her gently but firmly away from the parked car and up the deserted road. The restaurant was almost at the end of the last line of chalets before the meadows, and ahead of them moonlit snowfields gave way to snow-dusted pine forests.

They walked in silence, the only contact between them his restraining hand on her arm when the road got icy. Before them on the moonlit track their shadows fell, side by side. Now that they were outside the warm restaurant, full of the murmur of voices, the world seemed to contain only the two of them.

It was almost with the shock of awakening from a dream that Fiona realised that they had come to a standstill and that she was looking up into Dr Eckhart's face. It was exactly as it had been that other moonlit night, when she had fled from the dance floor and Erich's kiss. She shuddered as she recalled that night . . .

Then she felt Dr Eckhart's arms go about her, drawing her closer and closer into his embrace. She felt the soft thickness of his sheepskin coat, and beneath it the broad strength of his chest. He held her tightly to him for what seemed an eternity, and then very slowly released his hold. She felt him stroking her hair and then his fingers gently caressing the skin at the nape of her neck.

All of her feelings were focused on the places on her

body where his hands touched her, discovered her. Every nerve responded to his touch as if it had been waiting a lifetime for it. He caressed her as if he had practised this embrace; as if her body were almost familiar to him.

At last he found her lips and Fiona felt his mouth once more upon her own. But this was different from the first time that he had kissed her. This time there was no mistaking his hunger, his desire for her. She felt his passion and the answering tide rising in herself. She returned his kiss, at first passively but increasingly urgently, feeding it with the feeling that she had contained for so long.

She caught her breath. She could feel her heart moving against the slow, heavy beat of his. And then he held her away from him so that he could see her face.

'Thank you, Fiona,' he said softly. 'Thank you.'

His voice was deep with desire. Yet he was controlled, as if he himself had contained his own passion for a long time. Fiona felt herself stirred by his strength. His eyes were darkened in the moonlight. He seemed totally inaccessible now that the moment when she had been closest to him was past.

They walked silently back to where the Mercedes stood majestically in the moonlight and Fiona wondered incoherently whether Hans had been truly thanking her for her first month as his clinic Sister. But she did not believe that.

Outside the clinic he stopped the car and escorted Fiona up the steps to her flat. She found her key and opened the door, uncertain whether or not he expected to be invited in.

'It was a wonderful meal . . . everything . . .' she began.

But he bent and brushed her cheek with his lips, silencing her.

'I shall see you tomorrow, before I leave, Fiona,' he promised. 'Goodbyes must be left until the last moment.'

She watched him get back into his car. The Mercedes purred gently away.

CHAPTER SEVEN

FIONA was awoken from deep and peaceful sleep by the ringing of her telephone. At first she thought she must be dreaming, but then she was forced to pull herself from between the warm sheets, wrap her bathrobe around her with heavy limbs and glance at the alarm clock. It was just before six a.m.

'At last! Is that you, Fiona? I thought you were never going to answer.'

The sound of Daniel's voice had the effect of cold water being poured over her. She stiffened and increased her hold on the receiver until her knuckles showed white.

'Daniel! Where are you?' she asked, with dread.

'In Elchester. But not for long. I'm flying out in a couple of hours time. I thought I'd let you know.'

'Flying out? Here?' Fiona echoed.

'Well, you don't sound exactly overjoyed to hear me. Why didn't you answer my letter? Got fed up waiting for you to reply and decided more drastic action was required.'

The familiar chuckle filled her with alarm and pain in equal parts.

'But you can't come here, Daniel,' she said quietly. 'There is no point. I didn't answer your letter because I had nothing to say to you.'

'Listen, old girl, I know, I know. We need to talk face to face. I'll be with you later today. Longing to see you. Take care . . .'

'You'll waste your journey, Daniel,' Fiona said. But as she spoke she heard the receiver click down at

Daniel's end and the answering deadness at hers.

A sense of outrage and helplessness swept over her. How dare he be so presumptuous? The thought of him invading her privacy here, of him polluting her new-found Alpine peace with his brash assumption that she was his for the asking, made her furious.

She put the kettle on to boil and stepped into the bathroom. Beneath the comforting warmth of the shower she consoled herself with the thought of last night. How lovely—how perfect the evening had been. She was beginning to accept that to love this man was her fate and that she must accept as a bonus what blissful moments of recognition he gave her.

After all, her life could be a good deal poorer than that which opened up before her now. She was living in one of the loveliest parts of Europe and she had her own pretty home. She was financially better off than she had ever been, and the Weiss Kreuz Klinik offered her challenging and satisfying work. Professionally she admired and respected her colleagues. She had more than most women of her age.

She dressed in one of her crisp white uniform dresses and then sat down with her tea. Perhaps it was just as well that she had been awoken early. Hans had said that he would see her before he left for Geneva. This way she could be in the clinic first thing and be sure not to miss him.

She told herself that it was ridiculous to want to see his face again before he went away for a week. She told herself that a week was no time at all, that it would pass quickly and that she would find plenty to do. But she knew that the hours that she did not spend working would hang heavily on her hands.

The thought of the week stretching ahead led her back to Daniel's phone call. She shivered involuntarily and looked out at the quiet blue early morning sky which heralded another fine Alpine day. He would not come. He could not come.

Fiona washed up her cup and saucer and slipped into her duty shoes. It was still only a quarter to seven, but she would go down to the clinic. There would be plenty that she could do before the first patients began to appear.

She had made many small but important changes in the nursing organisation of the clinic since her arrival. These changes had gone unrewarded in terms of praise from her medical director, and attempts to make sweeping changes had always proved counter-productive. But all this Fiona now accept calmly. The young medical assistant, on the other hand, greeted all improvements with enthusiasm and compliments.

Fiona, while she shrank from the extravagance of his praise, was quietly encouraged in her professional belief in herself. Inwardly she knew that whatever the reasons for Dr Eckhart's strangely negative attitude to her work sometimes, it was not based on any rational assessment of her usefulness. She kept her chin up and privately set herself the task of convincing him.

Every day provided new opportunities for doing so. She worked long and careful hours, adjusting the running of the clinic better to meet the needs of its clients. Renata congratulated her upon the swift treatment of minor injuries, the thoroughness of the new follow-up procedure and the efficient renewal of surgical supplies. Fiona's confidence grew.

On Monday mornings she routinely checked and ordered new bandages, splints and Tubegauz for the plaster room, and today was no exception. She never ceased to be amazed at how much they got through. The thought made her smile; if she had proved herself in no other way in these few weeks, at least Dr Eckhart now accepted her ability in this area.

Stacking row upon row of different sized Tubegauz, Fiona found herself remembering their first clinical encounter. She recalled with a small thrill of fear his dark figure looming out of the snowy darkness of the forest path upon which she had fallen. She remembered the warm safety of his arms and the close comfort of his broad chest as he had carried her down the mountainside. And she remembered his quiet apology when later she had told him of her professional status.

She knew better now than ever to mention her nursing predecessor here in the clinic. The fact that there had been one lay between herself and her colleagues secretly and silently, like uncharted territory. Fiona suspected that something terrible must have happened; something that had so shaken the medical director of the clinic that he still could not bring himself to talk about it. A tragedy? Perhaps there had been some disastrous professional blunder involving a patient. That would explain Dr Eckhart's lack of total trust in her; his fear of changes that might lead to other mistakes being made.

As if to remind her of the possibility of clinical errors, Renata called through at that moment to tell her that the Colles' fracture was back for her first follow-up appointment. Fiona gasped. She had made that appointment and it had been for nine o'clock. The hours had already flown by.

'Come this way, Mrs Bowman,' Fiona said. 'That looks fine.'

'I'm sure there were some pins and needles in my forefinger. Not bad enough to come back with, but, you know . . .'

Fiona examined the hand carefully, but the fingers that emerged from the plaster cast were pink, mobile and unswollen. She did not have to wait long for the real cause of the woman's disquiet.

'I can't believe I paid all that money for a skiing

holiday just for this to happen,' she said, eyeing her plaster cast with some disgust—as if it had nothing to do with her.

'I sympathise,' said Fiona with feeling. 'I fell and hurt my ankle on my first skiing holiday and lost almost all my second week.'

'Did you, dear?' Her patient looked at her with renewed interest. 'Well, I bet you've made up for it since. What a lovely place to live and work!'

'Yes,' said Fiona. 'I am lucky, aren't I?'

And she knew that she was. She knew that she had everything to be happy about and nothing to worry her, and yet . . . While she made a second appointment for Mrs Bowman, she screwed up her courage to ask the receptionist whether Dr Eckhart had left any message for her. She must have missed him somehow.

'These efficient recalls you have arranged, Fiona,' said the receptionist.

'Efficiency!' Fiona smiled as best she could and tried to keep her tone light and bright. 'I feel as if I've been on duty for three days already! Has Dr Eckhart been in, Renata? I wondered if he'd looked in on his way off to his lecture tour.'

Renata looked surprised.

'No,' she said. 'He was leaving very early. I wasn't expecting him to look in before he left Wengen.'

'No,' Fiona responded, 'of course not. Why should he?'

So that was that. He had promised so ardently that he would see her before he left. It was unimportant, of course, merely a gesture on his part. But it would have meant so much more to her than that.

Renata reappeared, having apparently popped in to the treatment room in which Dr Franz Wilhelm was stitching a cut finger to check that he hadn't seen the medical director either.

'No,' said the receptionist. 'He went straight from home to the station. He hasn't been in here.'

'Thank you, Renata,' said Fiona. 'It was just a thought . . .'

'Was it something important?' asked Renata. 'I can contact him via his hotel in Geneva.'

'Oh, no,' said Fiona, feeling as if the whole thing was now completely out of proportion. 'It was nothing, honestly. Nothing at all.'

She managed to smile at her friend before calling the next patient.

She was glad for the stream of patients who poured through from reception into the consulting room all morning. She was glad for Dr Wilhelm's cheerful smile and candid appreciation of her help. And she was sorry when she realised that she would have to spend lunch-time alone, for Renata and Dr Wilhelm stepped out of the clinic, discreetly hand in hand, on the dot of one o'clock.

It was unusual for them both to go out at lunch-time. Although Renata was allowed a conventional break from work in the middle of the day, and patients seemed to honour this period too, unless they absolutely had to come in during it, the clinic staff normally ate together. They normally spent a pleasant hour or so chatting and drinking coffee in the little room off the reception hall, while Dr Eckhart went home.

But now Fiona found herself alone in the clinic. She had no appetite. She made herself a cup of coffee and took it out to a table in the hall. Staring at the wisps of steam that rose from the cup, then disappeared into the air, she forced herself to admit to the transient nature of human passion. She knew that it was stupid of her; she could not understand why she had set so much store by Hans' promise to say goodbye to her today. After all, a week was not a very great time. Yet the betrayal of his promise cut her. It seemed to invalidate so many of his words. It seemed to negate the few precious moments of intimacy that they had shared.

Fiona sipped her coffee and it scalded her throat. She put the cup down, but tears had already gathered behind her eyes in response not to the pain in her throat but to something else. That kiss! He must have thought her easily bought. A wave of shame washed over her.

She was going to need a lot of dignity to outlive that moment. Perhaps it was Daniel's phone call acting on her subconscious, reversing the effect it had had upon her before, but now she thought of home. In the park between Monmouth Gardens and St Helen's Hospital the softly shaded tips of purple, white and yellow crocuses would be pushing their way up through the soft earth. The grass, faded from its winter rest, would be darkening and the fresh green shoots of daffodils gathering beneath the still bare trees.

How she had always loved the spring in England! She pushed aside the notion that she was running away from Wengen. She persuaded herself instead that a weekend in Elchester would restore her calm and commitment to the clinic here. She had enough money to fly home whenever she had the time and inclination. When Dr Eckhart returned she would tell him that that was what she wanted to do—and she'd ask for the couple of extra days which she'd earned off in lieu of overtime she'd put in during his lecture tours.

Fiona finished her coffee and stood up. She felt slightly better, although the desolation which had settled itself at the pit of her stomach remained. Returning from washing her cup she found a tall, slim figure waiting for her in the hall.

'Hi! Fiona!'

Erich grinned broadly. Fiona surveyed the suave figure in the dark blue ski suit coolly. Erich looked pleased with himself—a very different picture from the one he had presented last time she had seen him in here. Her mind flew to Sue and Janice. The ski instructor had looked less than confident that day. She recalled the fury with which her employer had dressed him down. She had been embarrassed at her inability to avoid overhearing what had been said.

But somehow now she no longer felt like that.

'What can I do for you?' she asked. She was aware of wanting Erich to be gone from the clinic, as if her own slight lack of regard for him had been greatly reinforced.

'You are so serious. When I see you here I get your professional face, huh?' Erich lifted his eyebrows in mockery and Fiona felt a surge of anger at his contempt for her position at the clinic.

'That is to be expected,' she said, with annoyance, too, at her own prim tone. 'I am on duty.' She could well have done without this social call.

'Fiona, come! There is nothing to be cross about. I want you to come for a little meal with me, perhaps a fondue? I can promise you the best in Wengen . . . or have you forgotten? No. You have not forgotten.' He smiled ingratiatingly.

Fiona stared into the empty blue eyes. She looked at the silken blond hair and it suddenly looked effeminate in a way that it had not done before. Erich was totally devoid of attraction for her today.

'Thank you, Erich, but no thank you,' she smiled.

He shifted uncomfortably and his smile became somewhat fixed.

'What have I done?' he asked with an innocent shrug of his shoulders.

Fiona was not sure, but she was angry.

'I expect the skiing population of Wengen is diminishing,' she remarked, 'and that your choice of evening companion must have followed suit.'

'That is not very kind,' he muttered. But at least he had the grace to colour slightly.

'No. I don't suppose it is,' said Fiona. 'Goodbye, Erich.'

He shrugged again with exaggerated resignation, then lifted his hand in a farewell salute.

'Sorry about how you feel,' he said, 'but *au revoir*.'

Fiona watched until he had disappeared on the road. He didn't give a damn, she thought. He probably hadn't given her a thought for weeks. He issued invitations at whim, when and to whom it suited him. What a pig! No wonder Dr Eckhart had no time for the man. Somewhere inside her, Fiona felt relief that she had liberated herself at last from the urge to accept any offer of male companionship. But she knew the reason why, too, and she could not hide from that.

As if in answer to her prayer for work to take her mind off this train of thought, an old man hobbled in through the double doors. He looked taken aback by the device that automatically opened the inner ones, and Fiona stepped forward quickly to take his arm. It was strange to admit one of the townspeople to the clinic. She was so used to the international gloss of her skiing clients that it was a shock to meet rural simplicity in a patient.

She greeted him in her still stumbling German and then rapidly assessed the damp pallor of his skin beneath the grime. Wrapped around the hand and wrist of his left arm was a filthy rag through which spread the dark stain of fresh bleeding. The old man gestured feebly at his hand and tried to smile. He was calm, but obviously shocked.

Fiona led him to the first consulting room, mentally busy with the first aid that she would administer and the hope that Franz would not be late back from lunch. Gently laying the old fellow down on the examination couch, she heard the welcome sound of her two col-

leagues. It was just as well. She unwound the rag and a
spurt of bright red arterial blood leapt up at her. Grabbing a tourniquet from the trolley beside her, she tight-
ened it around the patient's upper arm. The spurting
stopped. She glanced at her watch to check what time
the pressure had been applied above the bleeding artery.

The old man's eyes followed her while she loosened
the neck of his shirt, then checked his pulse and blood
pressure. He was calm with age and amused confidence
in this new-fangled technology that surrounded him.
Looking into his face, Fiona recognised the old woodcutter whom she had met on her occasional early morning walks. She imagined that he spent his summers up in
the mountains gathering and cutting wood to sell. This
accident must have happened down here for him to have
got into the clinic on his own two feet.

A ragged saw wound opened blackly in a deep trans-
verse line from the base of his thumb to that of the third
finger. It would need careful repair. She began a preliminary cleaning of the surrounding skin and was glad to
see Dr Wilhelm appear at her side.

'Hallo! *Grüssen*,' he greeted the woodcutter gently.
The old man shook his head, smiling up at the young
doctor whom he had known since he was a little boy
playing in the village streets. The older man's trust in the
younger was complete.

Dr Wilhelm found and sealed the bleeding artery
and Fiona released the tourniquet she had applied. A
moment later she watched the faded blue eyes
of the woodcutter slowly close into a light sleep of
resignation.

Meticulously, the young doctor began to snip away
tags of torn tissue, bringing the edges of the ragged
wound gradually into alignment for stitching.

'It *is* a nasty one,' he murmured.

'Thank goodness he was down here when it happened.

He might have bled to death up in the mountains,' Fiona replied, handing Dr Wilhelm a fine black silk suture.

'Many men, and young men too, have died from such injuries working on the land,' he said. 'It is very bad how many, before this clinic. The great, how do you say, knives for the hay?'

'Scythes,' said Fiona softly.

'The great scythes that must be used still on the steep fields where the machinery cannot go. They caused much injury and death.'

'So the skiers have meant that now there is a clinic and injuries like this one are treated in time?' Fiona voiced her thoughts. At the same time she reminded herself that the woodcutter would need some anti-tetanus toxoid and an antibiotic to keep infection at bay.

'Yes, exactly,' Dr Wilhelm responded. He paused, then went on in a quiet voice, 'For me is it a very great thing to be able to sew this old man's hand. He and my greatfather?'

'Grandfather,' Fiona corrected him.

'They farmed together for many years. And then both my own father and Dr Eckhart's father worked the land in these mountains too.'

Fiona glanced swiftly up at the absorbed features of the young doctor as he placed another perfect suture.

'For some reason,' she said quickly, 'I had assumed that Dr Eckhart was a newcomer to Wengen.' Hans' name seemed to catch in her throat and then to sing in her ears like a bird rejoicing in its new-found freedom.

'No,' said Dr Wilhelm, giving her a careful look. 'He is very much a local man.'

A neat line of twenty black stitches marched across the woodcutter's palm like an army of busy ants. The papery skin was puckered and reddened, but each finger moved at Dr Wilhelm's instruction. The nerves and tendons had miraculously escaped injury. A slow smile spread over the old man's face as he thanked the doctor.

'One millimetre deeper and . . . *kaput!*' Dr Wilhelm straightened his back and smiled too. The woodcutter shook his head again as if the whole episode had had more to do with God than man.

While the doctor gently bandaged a dressing over the wound, Fiona allowed herself to think about his words. So Dr Eckhart was a local man. She had been very wrong in her assumption that Hans was simply making a comfortable living here during the winter sports season, giving the odd lecture and then probably taking the summer off. She had been far from generous in her suppositions. She had never considered the possibility . . .

'He has turned down many important professional opportunities and a potentially brilliant future in academic surgery in order that he might stay here, among his own people, to help them,' Dr Wilhelm quietly explained. 'He is a rather, er, remarkable man,' he stated simply.

'Yes,' said Fiona when she had found her voice and her poise once more. 'Yes, I see that he is.'

She thought of the beautiful house on the side of the mountain, the big car and the apparent comfort of his life. The thought that he was here purely for love of the people had never crossed her mind before.

But now she thought for the first time about them and about how the village must have lost its innocence. She pictured the pylons stretching up the mountainsides and the faces of the simple people who had swapped work on the land to provide service in the hotels and restaurants. And her heart was moved at the realisation of the changes they had seen.

Suddenly she seemed to understand. Suddenly an English spring had lost its appeal and she found herself longing instead for her first Alpine one and wondering how the mountains would look returned to their more rightful owners.

She put her hand gently on the woodcutter's shoulder and led him out to the reception hall.

'You'll have to come back to have those stitches out, and I'm afraid there's too many for just one session,' she smiled at him.

He smiled back at her and shook his head. He did not understand her German.

'Renata, please could you explain to this gentleman that he must come back in a week so that we can look at his hand and perhaps take out some of the stitches? My German is still so bad . . . Renata! What on earth is it?'

The receptionist was blushing a deep pink. She took the folder of notes from Fiona though, and as she did so Fiona saw the reason all too clearly. A brilliant diamond shone on the third finger of her friend's left hand.

'Oh, Renata, *Glückwunsch*!' she exclaimed. At least she knew how to congratulate her friend. She took her face in both hands and kissed her lightly on both cheeks. 'I am so happy for you,' she told her.

'*Danke schön*,' Renata returned, and the old woodcutter shook his head again and smiled at the two girls.

'So that's what you went off to do this lunch-time,' Fiona grinned. 'I should have known. Slipping out like that without a word!'

'I did not mean it to look like that,' Renata said, suddenly afraid that she might have upset Fiona. 'But we only decided last night. I'll tell you later . . .'

The receptionist turned her attention to making an appointment for the woodcutter, and Fiona tried to turn hers away from the sparkling stone upon Renata's hand. It seemed to light the whole room. Fiona knew that Renata's words had not been strictly true. Franz had been proposing to her for a long time, even to Fiona's knowledge, but Renata had at last decided to accept his offer of marriage.

She went to congratulate the medical assistant, thinking that last night had certainly been an occasion for some. As far as she was concerned, the moonlit snow, the silvery mountains and Hans' arms around her seemed like a dream from which she had now truly awoken. She wore no diamond ring to make it real for her.

It seemed, to judge from these two, so easy to be happy. Why was her destiny so different?

She came back to reception and smiled at Renata.

'You won't be leaving the clinic when you get married, will you?' she asked.

'No. At least not soon, I hope,' Renata replied, blushing again.

'And Franz?'

'No. Also not. But we have been so nervous of telling Dr Eckhart of our plans in case he felt it would be bad for our work. Yet we do not see how this can happen.'

'Of course not,' said Fiona, surprised. 'Why should your work suffer simply because you have got married?'

A strange expression came into the receptionist's eyes, one that Fiona recognised from the past. She remembered slowly when it had been—the evening that she had been crying, so soon after her arrival. This was that same evasive expression, one that was so foreign to Renata's pretty, open face. And it had been in connection with the conversation about how Dr Eckhart resisted changes in the nursing organisation of the clinic.

'The doctor has his own reasons for his fears,' said Renata now, confirming Fiona in her recollection. 'Personal reasons.'

Fiona felt the conversation closed as firmly as it had been all those weeks ago under similar circumstances

But now her response was different. She wanted to know what lay beneath her employer's strange prejudices

Later, she could not think what had made her look outside at that precise moment. The clinic was still. They had seen no new patients since the woodcutter had hobbled out, and now it was after three. But when she did look, the sight that met her eyes stopped her thoughts and her heart.

Daniel Davenport was outside, his hand outstretched towards the doors, a suitcase in the snow at his feet. His other hand was extended towards a beautiful blonde who was being pulled in an opposite direction by an all too familiar dog. Daniel was smiling charmingly at his lovely guide while she looked into the clinic and met Fiona's stare with triumph stamped across her face.

Fiona felt the blood leave her legs. What in the world was he doing with her? Fiona swallowed, steadied herself and applied herself to meeting him calmly. She leaned against the reception desk, glad of Renata's innocent presence.

'Hello! How are you, my love? You look as gorgeous as ever!'

Daniel had not changed either. He planted his suitcase firmly upon the marble floor and stepped towards her. Renata gazed in amazement at the Englishman and Fiona saw him for a vivid instant with her eyes—a tall, handsome Anglo-Saxon stranger, clear-eyed and fresh-faced as the schoolboy he had once been. His clean good looks had struck Fiona an almost physical blow when first he had strolled into Operating Theatre One at St Helen's Hospital, and now she saw the same effect produced upon her friend.

'I . . . I'm fine, Daniel,' she said, summoning all her self-control, 'How are you?'

'Amazing! All the better for seeing you '

For a terrible moment, Fiona thought that he was going to kiss her, but mercifully he was far too aware of the effect that his presence was having upon the pretty blonde behind the reception desk for any such demonstrations of affection.

'Well, aren't you even going to offer me a cup of coffee? I fly all the way here to see you and offer you my hand . . .'

Fiona saw the small smile that passed across Renata's face. She had to get rid of Daniel.

'Renata,' Fiona thought quickly, desperate to get himself out of this situation which could so easily be misread, 'would you mind awfully if I took the rest of the afternoon off? I'd like to talk to my, er, guest.'

'Of course,' said Renata, her face carefully blank.

'If anything comes up and you need me, I'll be upstairs. But things are so quiet, I feel you can do without me at present.'

Fiona tried to appear off-hand about Daniel's appearance, but it was difficult. She hoped that Renata would prove to be her usual discerning self and would appear later that evening for a cup of English tea and a chat. But she knew that the receptionist had other things on her mind today.

Upstairs in her flat, Daniel looked about him admiringly and flung his coat over the back of a chair as if making himself at home. Fiona wasted no time on pleasantries. She made coffee in silence and handed him his cup without a word.

'Lovely,' said Daniel, slightly put out. He had clearly expected a warmer reception.

'I told you that you would waste your journey, and that was what I meant,' Fiona stated.

'Fiona,' Daniel began placatingly. She had heard this tone before. And so often before she had melted. She had accepted the hollow excuse and the empty apology.

'It's no good, Daniel. We have nothing to discuss.'

'Fiona, about Kelly . . .'

The name was a trigger to Fiona, and she exploded. 'Don't you "about Kelly" me,' she declared. 'I couldn't care less about Kelly—or about you, for that matter. Leave me alone, Daniel. I'm happy without you in my life.'

To her surprise, her words had the reverse of the desired effect upon her ex-boyfriend, who seemed to respect her new-found assertiveness far more than he had ever respected her passivity.

'I quite understand how you must feel,' he said meekly. 'I know how things must look to you. If only you could know how sorry I am; how much I regret my treatment of you.'

This speech was so obviously sincere that Fiona almost found herself relenting. But she stuck to her resolve.

'Fiona, I want you to marry me. Please consider it, at least. I can't get you out of my mind.'

Fiona thought bitterly of the days and weeks of torture that she had suffered on account of this man. So now he couldn't get her out of his mind! Well, now he knew what it had been like for her.

He came towards her and while she was still immersed in angry thought his arms went around her and his face came close to hers. He kissed her easily, softly at first, in spite of her resistance, and then with force. Fiona was horrified at the alien, unwanted pressure of his mouth on hers. She pulled away from him with all her strength, anger lending power to her arms.

'Daniel, I want you to go. Now.'

'Fiona, please forgive me.'

He looked utterly wretched, but Fiona felt no pity for him. She scanned his face, wondering what she had ever seen in it to love.

'I'm sorry too,' she said with dignity. 'I didn't want to have to be rude to you.'

'That's all right,' Daniel said, the beginnings of a sheepish smile upon his face. 'It's called role reversal.'

At this moment, when he was meekest and weakest, Fiona was shocked at how unattractive she found him.

'I know I'm asking a lot of you, Fiona, but that has never been too much before—professionally or personally.'

Fiona shrugged at the attempted compliment.

'I'll wait around to give you time to think over what I've said. I'll book into an hotel.'

It struck Fiona that this last was an afterthought, and that actually Daniel had expected to sleep at her flat.

'It wouldn't matter if you waited a year,' she said. 'I should still not change my mind. But I know you, Daniel, and you will do what you want to do. Only please don't disturb me at work again. The clinic is really not the place to conduct private conversations and I'd appreciate it very much if you'd respect the position I hold there.'

Daniel nodded absent-mindedly.

'I had no intention of coming to the clinic at all, but I realised that you wouldn't be home yet and, anyway, I didn't know where the flat was. Luckily, I met this gorgeous blonde who not only spoke excellent English with a lovely sexy accent, but knew who you were and seemed only too happy to conduct me to the clinic—especially when I'd told her that I was your expected fiancé. I know it's a bit cheeky—but not too far out of true, eh?'

Fiona gasped. It was bad enough that he had managed to get one of the secretaries in Administration at St Helen's to betray her confidence and give away her address, but that he had persuaded this woman, of all the people that she least wanted to know of his presence here . . .

'You told her *what*?' Fiona said very quietly.

'What's up? It isn't that bad, Fiona, all things considered.'

She scanned his bland, uncomprehending features and hated him. He was so stupid, so juvenile and so insensitive that it was a mystery to her how he had qualified as a surgeon. How had he managed to convince anybody that he understood human beings in the least, let alone cared about them?

'Get out, Daniel.'

'I'll let you know where I'm staying,' he said, hardly able to get the words out quickly enough. 'I'll drop a note through your door or something.'

'Don't bother. Goodbye, Daniel.'

'*Au revoir* . . .'

Fiona shut the front door behind him with a bang and then leaned against it until his footsteps had disappeared. Almost the moment that they did so, her anger converted itself into tears and loneliness. How dare he come here? How dare he gossip about her with strangers? It was too much.

Fiona was no longer a stranger to her innermost feelings though, and she admitted to herself that most of her misery was caused by the knowledge that Daniel's presence here would be faithfully reported to Dr Hans Eckhart. She thought of the triumph she had seen in the icy blue eyes of the blonde. It would have been plain to a far less sensitive witness how much she welcomed Fiona's 'fiancé'.

Fiona wandered into the kitchen with an ashtray in which Daniel had left the end of a cigarette burning. She thought of what terrible insignificance his presence here would be to her employer. Wrinkling her nose with disgust, she put the cigarette out and washed the ashtray and the two coffee cups they'd used as if the scene behind her could be thus erased.

She was unmoved by the distance Daniel had come to ask for her forgiveness; hadn't she had to come this far simply to rid herself of his infidelity? She was not stirred by his apparent remorse; she had suffered too much from his crocodile tears in the past. She would rather remain a spinster for the rest of her days than accept his proposal of marriage. What a day it had been! First Erich, with his sly, transparent invitation and then Daniel, penitent and pathetic with his proposal.

Outside, the last sunlight fell into the soft folds of the mountains, threw dark shadows . . . the Mönch and the of the Eiger, flanked by the Mönch and Jungfrau mountains threw dark shadows . . . the Mönch and the Jungfrau; the monk and the maiden.

For some reason Fiona translated them wistfully to herself for the first time. Perhaps it was the image that they suddenly conjured up of herself, working for the rest of her life beside Dr Eckhart, her love for whom would never be consummated. And yet she knew now, more than ever, that if that was how it must be, that was how it would be.

CHAPTER EIGHT

FRIDAY arrived painfully slowly. All week Fiona had worked hard, trying to immerse herself in clinic business and put her own unhappy affairs out of her mind. It had been difficult enough to do this during the daytime when she had been constantly reminded of other people's happiness by the unconscious joy that both Renata and her new fiancé seemed to radiate, but the evenings were even worse.

To her enormous relief, Daniel had at least honoured his promise not to come to the clinic. And although he had dropped a note of his address through her letter-box at the flat, he had not come to see her in person. She had not trusted him to leave her alone for so long. In fact, there had been moments when she had actually wondered whether she had badly misjudged Daniel, but always these thoughts had been banished by memories of his infidelity.

The evenings had seemed endless. She had come home late from work, tired out, sure that an hour of television was all that she needed to ensure herself the sleep of the dead. But instead she'd been barely able to concentrate on the films she'd tried to watch and had found her attention wandering constantly from the book she was reading. She had gone to bed only to lie awake hour after lonely hour wondering and worrying about Daniel, Hans Eckhart . . . everything.

As a result, she was tired and nervous. She knew that Dr Eckhart would be back today and that made her worse, so that when he walked into the clinic, a calm, suave figure in the same immaculate three piece suit and

139

raincoat in which she had first seen him, Fiona felt her hands trembling and her throat dry. Luckily, she had the opportunity to excuse herself from his presence immediately to examine a patient.

And he had nodded at her. That was all.

She blindly bound the dislocated shoulder of her patient with a figure-of-eight bandage. While she did so she talked to him, but she was speaking automatically, hardly aware of her own voice. She made a return appointment for him in the same way and then cast her eyes with relief around the empty reception hall.

'Coffee?' asked Renata.

At eleven o'clock the clinic was so quiet that it was hard to believe that this was anything but a calm before the storm.

'You look so tired,' Renata said. 'Are you not sleeping well?'

'No. Not really. I don't know why,' Fiona said vaguely.

'I thought you would be happy with your visitor?'

Then Fiona remembered that Renata had not come upstairs, as she had hoped, on the evening of Daniel's appearance. She was still under the impression that he was a welcome guest—perhaps even the reason for Fiona's tiredness.

The smile on the receptionist's face had turned to an expression of concern.

'No, Renata,' Fiona took the cup of coffee she was handed and sat down beside her friend. 'He is not the most welcome guest in the world. He was the main reason for my coming to Switzerland in the first place, and a good deal of my reason for staying here. I was in love with him once. But no more.'

'He was bad to you?'

'Pretty bad, yes.'

'I wondered if such a thing had happened to you,'

Renata said softly. 'I am sorry. He is still bad now?'

Fiona slowly shook her head.

'I don't know. He came back to ask me to forgive him and marry him,' she explained, 'but once bitten . . .'

The Swiss girl looked at her quizzically. 'He bit you?'

Fiona burst into laughter and after a moment of perplexed hesitation, Renata joined her.

'No,' Fiona managed between her giggles. 'It's another old English expression. "Once bitten, twice shy". It means . . .'

'It means that once one has been hurt in love, one is very, very careful that it does not happen again.'

The two women looked up at Dr Eckhart with surprise. They had not noticed him approach. His face showed none of the amusement that they had just shared.

'Is that not so, Miss Shore?' The doctor threw the remark at Fiona, his eyes cold.

'Yes, Dr Eckhart, that is precisely so. What a pity that you arrived only in time to hear the very end of our *private* conversation.'

She had the satisfaction of seeing the flicker of embarrassment which lit the flecked eyes for an instant.

'When your coffee-break is over, Sister, would you be kind enough to set up theatre for the cleaning and reduction of a compound fracture of the ulna? If and when you have time, naturally. I wouldn't like to rush you—but perhaps the patient would appreciate your prompt attention. And perhaps when you see the patient you will be only too keen to give it to him.'

Fiona shrank from the sarcasm in her employer's voice, but she put her empty cup down and stood up immediately in response to his words.

'All patients receive my prompt attention, Dr Eckhart,' she said with dignity. 'Where is he?'

'On his way. He is also suffering from some degree of

exposure and possibly concussion, although he does not remember losing consciousness. God knows how long he was lying up there before they found him . . . the idiot!'

Fiona heard his barely audible last word with amazement. She had never heard him refer to a patient with such lack of respect before.

Erich was brought down from the slopes of the Mönch, which he had been skiing off the *pistes*, in powder snow. He was still strapped to the rescuer's 'blood wagon' when they brought him in, a pathetic sight. He had fallen hard and slid a hundred or so metres down the mountainside until his progress had been abruptly halted by some rocks. He had protected his head with his right arm, and the sleeve of his ski jacket had been cut away by his rescuers to reveal bone shining whitely through a blood wound just below the elbow.

Erich was strong and fit, a natural athlete. He had the powerful arm and leg musculature of the experienced skier and the spare, hard physique of a natural climber As the surgeon commented drily to the anaesthetist, handing Betadine-soaked skin swabs back to Fiona as he did so, Erich used most of his physical attributes to their utmost. Only his grey matter escaped regular exercise.

Luckily for Erich, there was little or no damage to major vessels or nerves in the area of the fracture, but there was a large tear in the brachioradialis muscle which needed careful repair. Dr Eckhart worked quickly to reduce the fracture and insert a long intramedullary pin into the ulna, thus fixing it. The personal contempt in which he appeared to hold his patient would never have been guessed by the meticulous surgery he performed upon him.

But as he was closing the skin, he again addressed the

anaesthetist, so that Fiona could not avoid hearing what he said, standing as she was scrubbed up, between the two of them.

'This young man,' Dr Eckhart remarked, 'knows everything that there is to know about skiing—except when and where not to do so.'

He continued placing the tiny, perfect sutures.

'And that would not matter so much, were it not for the fact that he is an instructor, and people sometimes get hurt. Don't they, Sister?'

It was true, Erich was reckless, yet the anger in Dr Eckhart's eyes above his mask was more than that deserved by simple recklessness. Fiona began to remove the green drapes from Erich's motionless, supine body.

'Yes,' she agreed softly, 'it's true. They do.'

The surgeon thanked the anaesthetist, peeled off his gloves and then his gown and strode out of the operating room. Fiona accompanied Erich to the recovery area with the anaesthetist. They discussed the post-operative care of the patient, and then Fiona was left alone to sit with him until he was fully conscious.

She was exhausted by the time four-thirty arrived and Erich's anxious mother came to accompany her son home. A brother—a taller, less elegant version of Erich—was with her, and he helped get Erich into a waiting ambulance.

'Fiona,' he whispered, 'thank you for everything.'

'Don't thank me, Erich, just get better quickly,' Fiona responded wearily. She had reassured him and comforted him as he came round from the anaesthetic, and she felt drained by the experience.

She used the last of her energy to explain to his mother the observations that she should make regularly over the next twenty-four hours, in view of the uncertainty of Erich's neurological status. He had sworn that he had not been knocked out and his observations up until now

had given Fiona no cause to doubt his word. But she
wanted to be sure that he had no hidden head injury.

When she emerged from finishing cleaning, clearing
and setting up the operating room for possible emergency surgery, the clinic was deserted. She remembered
that Renata and Franz had said that they were going to
try to get away promptly at five because they were going
to spend the weekend with his parents in a neighbouring
valley.

Fiona could not help the pang of envy that pierced
her. Their weekend would be so different from hers. She
would spend hers alone again, while theirs would be
filled with friends, congratulations, celebration, toasts
and joy. She envied them, and yet she did not grudge
them their deserved happiness.

The thought of Renata's lovely ring brought back a
nostalgic image from her girlhood—the old advertise-
ment which had promised her, 'A diamond is forever'.
She had learned since then how elusive lasting love
really was. Yet the longing for a permanent partner lay
deep inside her like a dream which refused to fade with
day-break; a part of her very being.

She sat down tiredly behind the reception desk. As if
to mock her train of thought, Erich's name stared up at
her from the desk. Dr Wilhelm, in his haste to get away,
had thrown the case notes down without bothering to file
them. Fiona opened the buff folder to enter her own
nursing notes at the end of the pre- and post-operative
treatment and operation ones.

She picked up a pen and then remembered something.
For ages she had been unhappy with the way nursing
notes were crammed in at the end of those written up by
the doctors. For a long time she had been toying with the
idea of separating her record of the care she gave. She
had thought how useful it would be to build a system
which would provide an accurate, objective way of

measuring her contribution to the care of patients who passed through the Weiss Kreuz Klinik.

If nothing else, the exercise would be good for her morale. At best, she would convince the director once and for all of his wisdom in appointing her; at worst, she would at least perhaps convince herself. And in the absence of any convincing professional encouragement, that would be most welcome.

So she began work, fired with enthusiasm for her new task. She decided to date the new system from the first day that she had taken up post. The reception desk was soon piled with case notes which she pulled out of the red filing cabinet and placed in alphabetical order of surname in front of her on the long desk-top.

She decided to remove nothing from the old notes, but simply to transfer information to new nursing notes for each patient, which she would update as follow-up appointments were kept. She helped herself to a stack of blue folders from the stationery cupboard behind Renata's desk and began work.

First she described an evaluation of the care needed by the patient on admission, then a brief plan of his nursing needs, a description of the execution of the plan, and then an assessment of the care given in the light of the patient's condition at discharge.

The new notes would, she hoped, emphasise her attempts to individualise care, monitor any extension of her role to include procedures normally carried out by medical staff and provide a comprehensive record of her work from day to day.

She worked steadily, forgetting everything in her absorption in her task. She did not notice the clock move through five, six and seven o'clock. The darkness outside escaped her attention. She did not even stop for a drink. And she did not notice Daniel until he was beside her.

He had seen her from outside the clinic, a small, solitary figure, a red-gold halo of light from an angle-poise lamp at the desk bright in her hair. He had been filled with longing at the sight of her. And with the fear that his ex-lover would truly reject him, finally this time.

Fiona took a moment to adjust to reality. She took in Daniel's presence and the faint smell of alcohol on his breath with alarm, and stood up to meet him.

'I've been waiting to hear from you,' he said, holding his voice steady only with difficulty.

'Yes. I'm sorry Daniel. I should have let you know . . .'

'Well?' he said sharply. 'You've had plenty of time to think over my proposition. What do you think?'

Fiona pushed herself away from him until she was almost hard up against the filing cabinet. Behind her was the wall and the stationery cupboard door and her escape from him was cut off in front by the heavy desk. Although Daniel had not moved, she was filled with bounding, irrational panic at being alone with him in the deserted clinic.

'How about a cup of coffee?' she said, her bright tone sounding completely unnatural to her own ears.

'Upstairs?' asked Daniel.

'No,' she replied. 'Why not here?'

At least nobody would disturb them here. And upstairs there was the settee, the softly-lit sitting-room and the adjacent bedroom.

'The flat is cosier,' stated Daniel.

She sensed the tension in him. She had tested him too hard, hoping that there was a shred of decency left in him and that he would respect her decision as she had first given it to him. She had almost begun to hope that he had left Wengen without contacting her again.

She made coffee quickly and brought it to him at one of the marble tables.

'It's no, isn't it?' he asked wearily.

Could he really be going to make it this easy for her?
Fiona could hardly believe so. But she nodded.

'Why?' he asked dangerously.

'Listen, Daniel. You know what happened between
us as well as I do. You can't expect people simply to
recover from these things and pretend that it hasn't
happened. Their trust is destroyed . . .'

She wanted him to go. She wanted to finish the set of
notes that she was working on and then go upstairs to
bed.

'It was a terrible mistake, Fiona. Kelly was nothing.
She followed me . . .'

He was prepared to be disloyal to her now, just as he
must have been disloyal about her to Kelly.

'Daniel,' she said simply, 'goodbye.'

He stood up and she was again uncomfortably aware
of his extra inches; of the remembered strength of his
arms.

'I'm leaving tomorrow morning, Fiona. Come with
me? Or join me at Bristol in a couple of weeks? Please?'

She shook her head.

'No, Daniel. Goodbye.'

And then his arms were around her and she could not
escape from him. She smelled his familiar smell and was
sickened with the associations that it brought. She struggled to free herself from his embrace, but something
about him made her stop struggling. She felt his desper-
ation and a wave of pity washed over her, drowning
her resistance to him. She realised that she knew how he
was feeling and she felt herself relaxing.

He sensed her relaxation. Perhaps he sensed more,
for he found her lips and kissed her with practised ease,
expertly, so that Fiona felt all his old skill and knew how
seductive it had been.

She did not want him—but she longed for someone

. . . She did not want this kiss—and yet she ached to be kissed. Her mind was working too slowly to control a situation that was moving too fast . . .

'Sister Shore!'

The sound of her boss calling her name hit her like a bullet. She pulled herself from Daniel's arms and stood for a moment unsteadily, pushing her hair back from her face with both hands. The clinic was almost dark, but she had not dreamed that voice.

She spun round and found herself staring at the reception desk where, in the pool of light from the lamp, Dr Eckhart was searching furiously among the notes where she had been working.

'Where the bloody hell . . . ?' he exploded in English.

Fiona turned from her boss to Daniel.

'Daniel, would you mind going now?' she begged him urgently. *'Please?'*

'But we haven't finished talking . . .' His voice was level and confident again. He gestured insolently towards Dr Eckhart with his thumb. 'If you can give this good fellow a hand to find what he wants, we could go upstairs. You're off duty anyway.'

'She is *not* off duty, young man,' the older doctor told him, looking up from the chaos at the desk with livid features. 'Fiona, get the emergency box and come with me. What in hell's name has been going on here? Where are the notes for that young fool we patched up this afternoon? Erich Zimmerman?'

Fiona responded automatically, 'They must be in the filing cabinet,' and then she remembered that they were at the bottom of the pile on the desk. She ran over and dug them out for Dr Eckhart.

'I'll be in the car outside. Be quick. And lock up behind you,' he instructed her.

Fiona let herself into Dr Eckhart's consulting room and picked up the white tin of emergency medical equipment which was taken on domiciliary visits and to rescue operations. She had herself initiated the idea of this box, realising soon after her arrival that there was no such organised provision.

'Fiona!' Daniel blocked her path.

'Get out of my way, Daniel,' she declared, having completely forgotten his presence in the clinic.

'But, one word, Fiona. I'm off in the morning . . .'

'Daniel! For God's sake!' Fiona exclaimed. Not even a medical emergency moved him from his position at the centre of his own universe. He was incredible! This moment seemed to Fiona to say everything that there was to say about him, both the man and the doctor. She experienced an instant of burning shame at the scene that she had allowed to occur between herself and Daniel, and then she told him quietly that she never wanted to see him again.

He coloured too, and then seemed to recognise at last the seriousness of Fiona's words. He went out ahead of her and she locked the doors behind them both. The last she saw of him was his retreating back, his shoulders hunched angrily against the cold.

'Your other, er, friend is in trouble,' said Dr Eckhart distinctly.

His profile beside her in the car was granite. His grim mood seemed to originate deep inside him, where his anger had come from this afternoon.

'Erich?' she asked. 'What is the matter with him?'

Fiona flicked mentally through the care that she had given the ski instructor and recalled the measurements of pulse, respiration and blood pressure that she had recorded. They had been satisfactory enough. She had had no doubt about Dr Wilhelm's timing of the young man's discharge.

'You'll see,' the doctor replied.

She sat beside him for what seemed a long time while

the car slid through the quiet streets and then came to a halt outside a neat wooden chalet. Lights shone comfortingly at the windows, casting a warm glow on to the snow outside. But Fiona dreaded what she might find inside the cosy home. She wished with all her heart that she was sitting safely in her flat and that none of this evening had happened.

Her anxiety was well-grounded as things turned out. Erich was lying still, with closed eyes, upon a simple divan bed in the combined kitchen and living-room. His burly brother stood nervously smoking a pipe near the big, old-fashioned cooking range, while his mother came forward quickly to greet the doctor and the nurse. Her eyes were full of frank fear.

In rapid German, she explained that Erich had been fine until they had been home for about three hours, and then he had become restless before vomiting violently. She had been diligent in carrying out all the instructions that the nurse had given her, and when she'd got worried she'd telephoned the doctor, even though she didn't like to disturb him at home. Her son had not spoken for the last hour, and she couldn't rouse him to ask him how he was feeling.

Raised intracranial pressure: intracranial haemorrhage! The diagnosis banged around Fiona's own skull like a death sentence. Yet how could he be bleeding into his brain and she not have noticed it before? He had saved himself from the worst of the impact with the rock. Fiona visualised the violence of the injury to his arm. The force with which he had hit it must have been considerable. And behind his arm, the right side of his head must have been cradled in his elbow . . .

Of course. There could easily be a hidden fracture of the skull, possibly of the temporal bone. She struggled to recall the vital structures in that region of the skull while she took his pulse and measured the blood pressure. Dr

Eckhart, meanwhile, was carefully lifting each of Erich's eyelids in turn to look at his pupils and feeling gently and expertly around the head of his silent patient.

Fiona felt a slow, full and bounding pulse. She knew before she saw it the marked widening of pressure between the systolic and diastolic blood pressures which indicated further the certainty that pressure was rising inside Erich's skull.

He was slipping inexorably into unconsciousness. He was simply bleeding to death. Fiona fought to keep her features calm in the way that she had been trained to do. But inside she knew that he needed surgery, and fast. The only way in which his life could be saved now was by emergency surgery to tie off the bleeding vessel or vessels and drain the blood clot which was threatening to block the tiny vessels that fed the brain its life-sustaining glucose and oxygen.

She stayed beside him while Dr Eckhart used the telephone. He seemed to be out of the room for an eternity. Fiona smiled at the relatives calmly and reassuringly trying, in her broken German, to comfort them. But she could not hide the gravity of the situation from them, and she knew it.

It was a relief to hear the telephone receiver click down and have the surgeon back with them all. He addressed himself first in gentle tones to the mother and her other son and then to Fiona, in English.

'It's epidural—a haematoma. He's still bleeding, probably from the middle meningeal artery. I think there's a fracture of the temporal bone.'

He stopped for a moment, in response to her startled expression.

'No, no, it's okay,' he went on in a gentler voice. 'You couldn't have spotted it this afternoon. Strange things, these. Typical history. You get a bang on the head followed by momentary unconsciousness, but not enough for the patient to remember. Perhaps he doesn't even realise he's been knocked out. Then there's a so-called lucid interval which can last a minute, or hours, and during which no abnormality is evident. And then the trouble starts. Deterioration in vital signs and progressive loss of consciousness . . .'

An insistent noise interrupted the flow of Dr Eckhart's words and drew Fiona's attention away from what he was telling her. The noise became louder and louder, until it seemed to fill the room. Fiona's alarm was seen and allayed momentarily.

'A helicopter,' said Dr Eckhart. His voice hardened. 'I want you to go with him to Bern, Fiona. I've phoned and they're expecting him at the neuro unit there. I can't leave this place unattended, and you shouldn't have any problems. It's not far. There's a paramedic on board already; one of the guys from the air ambulance service who's used to cases such as this. But I'd like you to go along just in case.'

Fiona felt her heart thumping against her ribcage. She felt fully up to the responsibility professionally, but the flight . . . She had never flown in a helicopter before and she was terrified enough of normal aircraft. Her panic increased with the volume of sound from outside as the machine came down lower and lower over the chalet.

She tried reasoning with herself with some success. She must not let either herself or Dr Eckhart down. She had a job of work to do and she must do it.

'Fiona, you look pale. Are you all right?'

His voice was sharp and the use of her first name did nothing to soften his question. This was no moment for tender concern for the well-being of medical or nursing staff. Fiona stood up. She had just completed another set of observations on Erich. She knew from them that her patient was slipping deeper and deeper into coma.

'I'm fine,' she answered briskly. 'Where is the helicopter landing?'

'They'll put her down at the back, on the flat field behind the chalet.'

As he finished speaking, she heard the engine outside change, then rise and fall and stop. She swallowed involuntarily and pushed her hair back with both hands in her old, nervous gesture.

She could feel Dr Eckhart's eyes upon her. He was staring intently at her without blinking and for a long instant Fiona felt his whole attention focused upon her. She swallowed hard again and tried to smile, but she knew that only a nervous twitch of her mouth resulted from her efforts.

'Okay, Sister Shore,' Dr Eckhart said softly, almost under his breath, and Fiona was sure that he addressed the woman in her and not the nurse. She knew, but she had no time to feel his words. She turned and followed the stretcher in which Erich was being carried from the chalet.

The air ambulance crew were swift, skilful and impressive. Two or three minutes later, Erich had been secured carefully inside the helicopter for his journey to hospital. Fiona stood in the snow beneath the huge machine, grasping her box of instruments so that she felt as though all her energy was in the knuckles of her right hand.

There would be all the things she needed to monitor Erich already on board the aircraft. She knew that, but she wanted to use the same things that she had used all along so as to be able to accurately report the smallest changes. She tried to concentrate upon the task ahead.

The younger of the two-man helicopter crew arrived at her side and grinned at Fiona. He was curly-haired and handsome and apparently pleased at the prospect of a trip in her company. Fiona cursed herself for letting him see her wistful glance across the silent snowfields. Now he knew what was going on beneath her professional calm. Sure enough, he patted the gleaming silver and red belly of the helicopter.

'She's beautiful,' he laughed.

'Of course she is,' Fiona replied wryly.

She felt the young man's hand beneath her arm as she mounted the first step up into the aircraft.

'But not as beautiful as our Snow Sister,' he said.

Fiona smiled at the reassuring nature of his banter, although she was in no state to appreciate compliments. She had to stoop almost double in order to get into the body of the helicopter.

'Where do I sit?' she asked, trying to keep her voice light.

'Here, next to the patient's head.' The crewman helped her into a cramped place next to the window. He put the two halves of her seat-belt into her hands.

'Strap yourself in tight. And don't worry,' he smiled. 'You really are safe.'

Fiona managed a small smile to thank him for his help, and then she turned all her attention to Erich.

The ski instructor was by now completely oblivious to all the drama surrounding him. He looked deeply asleep and untroubled. Fiona watched him while the helicopter took off, lifting from the ground like a vast mosquito. She tried to keep her mind on him and off the low exchange of voices over the radio, the heavy hum of the huge blades upon which all their lives now depended. As the machine lurched sideways and the ground slid away from beneath them, she tried not to look down at the blue-white diamond-studded patch of earth that was Wengen.

The next half-hour was one of the longest of her life. It was just over fifty kilometres to Bern from Wengen, as the crow flies. Twice during the flight Fiona carried out a

full range of observations on Erich, beginning afresh
almost as soon as she had finished a set. She watched
his colour in the flickering light of the helicopter and
checked his pupils again and again with her torch.

She had a clear mental picture of what was going on
inside Erich's head. She did not need to see the skull
X-rays that would soon be taken to know, from what Dr
Eckhart had told her, of the growing purple mass beneath the right temporal bone, which was pushing the
midline structures of his brain out of their true position.

And Dr Eckhart had not needed the angiography and
brain scan which would also no doubt be carried out at
the hospital, to arrive at his diagnosis. It was this that
had impressed Fiona most about the last hour. She had
seen her employer arrive at a swift, firm diagnosis, and
act on it. She had realised that in this small isolated
place, they needed just such a superb diagnostician as
he; someone able to assess and refer life-threatening
cases such as Erich's. The ski instructor had, Fiona
knew, a fifty-fifty chance of surviving his haemorrhage—
provided the bleeding was stopped as soon as possible.

The myriad lights of the city appeared beneath the
helicopter and the machine swung around in the sky at a
sickening angle to the earth. Fiona held on to the strap at
her side and held her breath too. She concentrated upon
Erich's unmoving eyes and the next thing she knew they
were miraculously down. The helicopter came to rest on
a landing-pad on the roof of the hospital, which was
apparently base for the air ambulance crew.

A short journey by stretcher down steps and along a
corridor, and then Fiona was able to hand over responsibility for the patient to a team of white-gowned nurses
who manned the silent neurological unit. Erich was to be
taken to theatre almost immediately, yet there was no
sense of panic in the unit, which dealt daily with cases as
dire as this. Fiona could not help the sense of relief that

filled her as Erich was wheeled away from her.

She hoped with all her heart that all would go well for him. But her feelings seemed to be swamped by the exhaustion that she had held at bay for so long. She attempted for a moment or two, as she walked back up to the helicopter landing-pad, to work out what lay at the root of Dr Eckhart's evident mistrust and dislike of the patient for whom he had cared so brilliantly. But she could not cope with the puzzle that it posed.

For herself, everything that had ever happened between herself and the ski instructor had been cancelled out by the seriousness of his current condition, just as this evening she had seen a similar mechanism operating in her boss.

The helicopter flight back to Wengen was almost enjoyable. Maybe Fiona's fears was dampened by exhaustion, but she was able to appreciate the amazing moonlit views of the mountains from her window, and the flight seemed much shorter than the outgoing one.

She closed her eyes during the swerving descent into Wengen and then waited for the clamour from the blades above her to cease before she thanked and said goodbye to the pilot. Very soon she was back down safely in the snow and able to take a gulp of fresh air.

'Fiona!'

The familiar voice reached her before she caught sight of a bulky figure in a sheepskin coat who stood on the edge of the landing pad. As soon as she saw Dr Eckhart his parting words flooded back to her and her breath caught in her throat.

'Over here,' he called.

She walked slowly over to where he stood, his hands thrust deep into his pockets, just as she had so often visualised him. She caught the fleeting fragrance of his tobacco and felt the nearness of him. But, looking up into the calm features of her employer, she could find

nothing to confirm her memory of tenderness in the
intensity of his stare across the chalet room. Like so
many moments with this man, that too seemed destined
to join her secret inner store unsubstantiated.

'I thought I'd meet you,' he stated, 'and take you back
to the flat. It's late.'

Fiona realised that she did not feel sure of where-
abouts in the village the helicopter had put her down.
She had never found out where the landing-pad was.

'Thank you,' she murmured, 'very much.'

'How did it go?' He led her firmly towards where he
had parked the car, just as he had on the night of her own
accident.

'It was fine,' she heard herself saying. 'His vital signs
stayed steady during the flight and then he was going
straight to theatre when we got to the hospital. Everything seemed very much under control when I left him. I
hope he is okay.'

'Okay . . .' the doctor repeated softly. 'And are you
okay, Sister Shore?'

He turned to her and she thought he searched her face
with care. She tried to discern his expression in the
silvery moonlight which so strangely softened everything it lit. But she was tired, so very tired. She could not
trust her senses any more.

'I am fine,' she whispered.

The doctor shook the car key noisily free from the rest
of the bunch and Fiona shivered.

'I didn't know that you were afraid of flying,' he
commented.

'Yes,' she said, 'but I had more important things to
think about.'

She sank into the passenger seat of the car, glad of the
comfort, glad of the darkness and the warmth which hid
her from him.

'That was brave of you, Sister Shore.'

Fiona felt the neutrality of the remark; the hollowness of the compliment. She had closed her eyes for a mere second, yet now the Mercedes was gliding up the clinic drive and round to her apartment.

'You should sleep well tonight—if you are not thinking about something more important.'

The coldness of the doctor's words, laden as they were with insinuation, shocked Fiona awake. It seemed that she could not afford to relax her guard against this man. She knew that he was alluding to Erich or Daniel and she felt the familiar wave of shame and anger rising inside her. She found the catch, opened the door of the car and let herself out as the engine fell silent.

'Goodnight, Dr Eckhart,' she said distinctly. 'I hope *you* sleep well.'

She slammed the car door, which resisted her angry push. Then she climbed the stairs to her flat, listening all the time for the receding sound of the car. But it did not come and she was aware of the doctor waiting as she had left him, motionless behind the wheel.

Forcing her shaking fingers to lock her front door behind her, she heard the violent surge of an engine and felt the muted protest of tyres as they missed their hold on the snowy drive.

CHAPTER NINE

THE FIRST thing Fiona did when she got into the clinic the next morning was to telephone the hospital in Bern for news of Erich. Apparently the operation had gone well; the bleeding vessel had been tied off and the haematoma evacuated and now Erich was recovering consciousness under intensive care. While it was too early for optimism, the staff were fairly positive about his prognosis.

Fiona had gone to bed exhausted and had got up in much the same state, having mentally spent the whole night nursing Erich. Behind her frantic efforts to keep him alive there had been the cool, calm stare of her employer. It had been as though she had been fighting a last battle of some sort, and this morning she had traced the atmosphere of her dream back to Dr Eckhart's indifference towards her last night.

She always hated Renata's weekends off. She missed her ready smile and her company through the day. Now Fiona found herself longing for the first patient to arrive to take her mind off her own less than robust condition. The knowledge that she would share her weekend on duty with her employer brought her no pleasure.

Nine o'clock arrived and there were still no patients. Fiona, having prepared the consulting and plaster rooms and checked the theatre in her usual thorough way, sat down and stared at the pile of case notes that she had been working on when Daniel arrived last night. Daniel! Well, she had found one thing to rejoice about this morning after all. She was certain that she would not hear from him again.

At first in a desultory manner, but then with renewed enthusiasm, she began again with her reorganisation. She felt herself relaxing as she immersed herself, watching new order created as she produced the neat folders of nursing notes.

An hour or so passed before the familiar clumping of ski boots upon the unnatural terrain of the reception hall heralded the arrival of her first patient. She attended to him and then returned to her task. If the day went on as quietly as this, she might get to the middle of the alphabet . . .

'Ah, Miss Shore.'

If he calls me that once more while I am under his employment here, I shall address him as Herr Doktor, I swear it, she thought. She knew that her fragile state predisposed her to anger or to tears and that neither response could be relied upon to occur appropriately. This awareness, given the imperious tone of Dr Eckhart's voice, boded ill.

'How are we this morning?'

'*I* am fine. Thank you. A little tired, that's all. How are you?'

'I am fine. Fine.' His forced smile bore into her.

She stared unflinchingly into his face, waiting for him to continue whatever he had to say.

'Would you like to come into my consulting room? I'd like to have a word with you.'

Fiona reacted against this summons. She was not a schoolgirl and besides, she was alone on duty and nobody else was available to meet patients.

'I'd rather stay here, if you don't mind,' she said quietly. 'I'm sure that you can say whatever you want to say here. We are quite alone.'

'And feeling rather fragile, I would imagine.'

'Yes, actually, I am.'

'It must have been a somewhat heart-rending mercy

dash for you last night,' he smiled sardonically and scanned her face for signs of a response to his words.

She was shocked at his tone. What was he getting at?

'It was a terrible thing to have happened,' she said. 'Terrible for everybody.'

She tried to think about Dr Eckhart's gentle voice as he reassured Erich's mother, and to equate it with the words he was using to her now. But the two men would not merge.

'But most terrible for you, eh, Miss Shore?'

'No,' she persevered in level tones, 'most terrible for Erich.'

'Erich,' repeated the doctor. 'But your Erich is going to be all right.'

'I hope so,' said Fiona.

She knew that Dr Eckhart had himself rung the hospital this morning, because the sister in charge there had told her so. She knew that his professional concern for Erich was sincere. So why was he being so unpleasant to her about him? This display of ill humour was quite separate from professional feeling.

'It was lucky that we caught him in time,' the doctor began again, and Fiona steeled herself for whatever was to come. 'Of course, it would have been a very great help to have been able to find the notes filed away in their proper place when I needed them.'

Fiona's mind flicked back to the notes, thrown carelessly down at the desk by the junior medical partner yesterday, and the injustice of Dr Eckhart's remark hit her.

'There was no delay caused by loss of the notes,' she answered confidently.

'And what if you hadn't been here? It was long after you should have been off duty—God knows what you were doing here . . . What sort of delay would have been caused then? It could have taken me half an hour to find those notes if you hadn't been . . .'

It was true. Dr Wilhelm had been in the wrong in the first place, but then she should have filed the notes. Fiona felt the blood rise and fill her cheeks. The memory of herself and Daniel flooded back to her—and that stupid, unwanted kiss. She remembered what Dr Eckhart had seen.

'I'm sorry,' she said. Her apology did nothing to restore his calm.

'What the hell were you doing there anyway?' he demanded.

She prepared herself to explain about the notes . . .

'Making a bloody mess,' he answered himself.

'I'm reorganising the documentation of patients' care so that medical and nursing notes are separate,' she said quickly.

'The system which we use here,' Dr Eckhart interrupted bitingly, 'is more than adequate. I have not the faintest idea why you consider yourself and your contribution of such importance. The nurse here has always . . .' he stopped abruptly.

Fiona waited.

'The nurse here has always *what*, Dr Eckhart?' she asked.

He took a deep breath and seemed to make an effort to control himself. A shadow moved across his features and he shut his eyes. Fiona had to resist a strong desire to move towards him and to touch his face. She was suddenly terribly sorry that this exchange was taking place and she wanted to make amends, to alleviate the situation for them both.

She began speaking quickly, in a low voice, willing him to understand.

'I thought it might be possible to evaluate my contribution to the care of patients here,' she said. 'Far from feeling over-confident, I wanted to prove to you that . . . I wanted to prove my worth to myself as well as to you . . .'

He stared at her as if he hadn't heard her, and then shook his head with an expression that Fiona could not read.

'And do you have another neat excuse for your other behaviour? Your extramural activities of last night?'

His voice carried weary anger, as if he had made up his mind to speak to her about this, but now that he came to do so he could not be bothered to hear her out.

'I'm very sorry for that too,' she said truthfully. She knew that she was blushing again and she did not have time to prepare herself for his next words.

'It was a disgraceful sight.'

'I'm sure that it was.' She shrank from the distaste in his words.

'Well, what the hell did you mean by it?'

'I did not want him to come here,' Fiona began. 'I didn't wish ever to see him again after I left England. But he came and it was late and . . .'

'You couldn't wait to get upstairs to your own apartment, eh?'

It was utterly unreasonable. *He* was utterly unreasonable. Fiona suddenly knew that there was nothing she could do or say to stop this scene until Hans Eckhart withdrew from it of his own accord. He was angry for his own reasons. She knew that she was innocent of any misdemeanour great enough to warrant his onslaught and that all she could do was remain as dignified as possible while the attack continued. She felt tears gathering hotly behind her eyelids and tried to concentrate upon keeping them there until she had privacy in which to weep.

'Straight from the arms of one suitor to the rescue of another. A real little angel! I think it would be kindest of

me to release you from your contract so that you're free
to marry one of them. Well, what do you think?'

This was too much.

'Hans!' Fiona burst out. 'What are you talking about?
Why do you interpret everything I do in the worst
possible light? Why? You must know that I have no
intention of marrying anybody . . . now or ever!'

She did not dare to look at him. One heavy tear had
already fallen and she could hardly contain the flood that
threatened to follow it.

She heard him leave and relaxed in the merciful
silence that was left behind him. Now she allowed her
tears to fall, taking with them all the tension of the last
hours and days. Ten or fifteen minutes later she washed
her face and combed her hair back up into its shining
coil, and felt better for it.

She realised for the first time that day how dark it was
outside, and went to the doors. No wonder she had seen
no patients for so long. Snow was falling steadily in large
flakes and she could hardly see the road. Only the best
skiers would be out on the slopes in conditions such as
this.

Fiona settled back to her task again. She would show
her employer how serious she was about it and her work
here. Somehow, she would show him who she was. She
tried to detach herself from her feelings for him and see
more clearly the background to the scene that had just
taken place between them.

The episode with Daniel still embarrassed her, but
when she thought about it objectively she saw only an
unfortunate incident involving herself—off duty. She
was sorry that it had taken place in the clinic, but that
could not be helped now.

Her employer had no right to treat her like a wayward
schoolgirl. It seemed that she had more respect for his
personal relationships than he had for hers. She had

apologised genuinely for her apparent indiscretion.
With some degree of subjectivity, she now thought of
the blonde and blamed her for Daniel's safe arrival at the
Weiss Kreuz Klinik in the first place.

Fiona could never forget the presence of that beautiful
woman in Dr Eckhart's life and neither did she expect
ever to usurp that position. Why should he so resent any
man who showed the slightest interest in her? She filed a
set of notes forcefully. There were times when she
profoundly wished that he had good reason for his
apparent conviction that she was about to join the
serried ranks of ex-nursing wives.

She sat back from her work. With detached amazement, Fiona realised for the first time how different she
was from he woman who had arrived here a few short
weeks ago to learn to ski. She thought about that
woman, emotionally shattered after her affair with
Daniel and with no idea of what her future might hold.
She had pretended to herself that she could and would
live alone, but in her heart of hearts she had not believed
her own story. She had allowed her disenchantment with
Erich to grow only with reluctance.

She had taken on her post at the Weiss Kreuz Klinik
almost in a dream, with little sense of the reality of her
break with her past. And secretly, she now admitted to
herself, she had hoped all along that her handsome
employer would admire her. It was a relief to admit to
herself at last that she had hoped that he would fall
in love with her. Now she could start to live with the
truth.

He did not love her, but she would continue to try to
earn his respect as his Sister-in-Charge. She did not need
his praise to survive. She would learn to contain her need
for a partner in her personal life and to appreciate Hans
Eckhart in so far as he was a small part of it. She would
not show her feelings for him, however they grew,

because to betray them was to open herself to ridicule
and contempt. And suddenly she was not prepared to
open herself to that any more.

When she remembered the kiss that they had shared
after the meal, she found that the shame had gone. The
delicious meal and the atmosphere of the evening had
lead them both to forget their situations for a moment—
that was all . . .

Fiona could not believe her eyes. For a split second she
thought that she must be dreaming the scene before her.
But she wasn't. The desperate expression upon Dr
Eckhart's face told her that. And his arms were full of a
limp bundle which, when he finally came into the hall,
Fiona recognised as his little son. Close upon his heels
followed the willowy blonde, her fur coat carelessly
open and her face distraught.

Fiona looked down at the small pale face beneath the
coloured woollen cap as Dr Eckhart laid the child gently
on his examination couch. The child opened his eyes and
Fiona saw the identical flecks of dark grey which disting-
uished his father's. He was such a beautiful child. Fiona
could not bear to see him in such obvious pain, his eyes
so huge and frightened.

The father spoke to him in a low voice while he
removed the child's ski suit quickly and gently. The little
limbs were soon exposed and Fiona saw the cause of
Edmund's pain. His right knee was grotesquely swollen
and he cried out when his father touched it.

Fiona heard a muffled exclamation behind her and
turned to see that the woman had collapsed and was
kneeling on the floor beside the doctor's desk. Dr
Eckhart was beside the huddled figure in a flash, cradling
the lovely blonde head in his arms and whispering,
'Helga, Helga,' over and over again.

Fiona concentrated upon taking little Edmund's pulse

so that she could not hear the doctor's murmured en-
treaties to the woman to collect herself. When Fiona
turned next, she saw that the blonde was standing,
leaning heavily upon Dr Eckhart, whose arm was about
her shoulders. He looked anxious—even annoyed.

'I've got to get back to the house for a little while,
Fiona. The other children are alone there. Can you
X-ray Edmund's leg for me? I don't think it's anything
but a tendon injury. He fell hard. I'll be back as soon as I
can.'

'Of course,' Fiona said. She was aware of noticing that
there was no wedding ring upon the blonde's finger, but
she hardly trusted her own senses. First Erich's terrible
injury, and now little Edmund lying before her . . .

'I'm going home for a minute, with Helga, Edmund,'
the doctor said gently. 'You'll be all right with Sister
Fiona, she'll take good care of you.'

He nodded at Fiona and then was gone. She turned
her attention back to her small patient in time to see a
flicker of pain pass across his features.

'We'll let you rest for a minute or two before we take a
picture of your knee, shall we? It must have been horrid
to fall on it so hard.'

She stroked his forehead, pushing the dark hair back
from his brows, and he closed his eyes so that his lashes
lay like tiny bird's wings against his pale cheeks.

'You're safe now,' she said.

'The snow was deep,' Edmund told her, opening his
eyes again and speaking clearly for the first time. 'It was
falling so I couldn't see where I was going.'

'Thank goodness you were found quickly,' Fiona said.

'Carl found me.'

Fiona raked her memory. *Carl*. She knew that name.

'Your big dog?' she asked.

'Yes. He was clever. He found me in the snow.'

'Well, when we've taken a photograph to make sure

that you haven't broken your leg you'll be able to go home with your papa and give Carl a special treat for his supper, to thank him. Or perhaps your mummy will already have done that . . .'

'My mummy's dead,' the child stated.

Fiona absorbed the words with silent shock, concentrating upon controlling her face.

'She got lost in the snow too. But she died.'

Fiona caught her breath as Edmund told her the truth with childish candour.

'Well, why don't we photograph your knee now?' she said. 'You can help me to put the plate under your leg. Would you like that?'

'It hurts if I move my leg,' Edmund told her, 'but I'll try. It's an X-ray, not a photograph.'

Fiona smiled at her little patient. She should have known better than to patronise him. Of course he knew what an X-ray was. For all she knew, he might have been introduced to the rudiments of orthopaedic surgery by now!

'I'm treating you as if you're a baby, aren't I?'

'No,' said the child frankly, 'you're lovely. Helga was angry with me when I was brought home. And then she started to cry.'

'I expect she was shocked and upset,' Fiona said, surprised at the generosity which she now felt able to offer the blonde woman.

'She's hopeless when any of us are ill,' said Edmund, matter of factly, as if the words were a familiar family truth.

Fiona wheeled the little boy through to the X-ray room and took four views of his knee. She was fairly confident of her ability as a radiographer by now, but this particular patient made her nervous. She wished his father was there. At the same time, she was amazed by the calm co-operation that Edmund gave her, helping her all he could and lying as still as a statue when she asked him to.

'Do you want to take an X-ray of my head, too?'

Fiona smiled at Edmund, sure that he was joking.

'Why should I want to do that?' she asked lightly. 'There's nothing wrong with your head, is there?'

'Well, I hurt it when I fell, and now it feels funny.'

A chill of horror ran through Fiona. 'How does it feel funny?' she asked quietly.

'I don't know. Just funny . . .'

She glanced hard at him, unable to believe what her training told her was about to occur. Yet her premonition, like his, was correct. Edmund lay still for a second longer and then went into the tonic stage of a *grand mal* seizure.

She grabbed the child with all her strength and managed to lift him bodily down from the trolley and lay him on the floor. There she placed him gently on his side in an attempt to stop him from inhaling secretions during the next stage of his fit, and moved a few things out of the way. As she did so, he stiffened and became cyanosed. He cried out as air was forced from his lungs by the sudden contraction of his chest muscles, and Fiona felt like crying herself at the suffering of the child.

All she could do was wait until it was over—and that, mercifully was not long. The little figure relaxed and Fiona gathered him into her arms at last. She felt him fall into the deep sleep that follows such a fit, feeling a tenderness for him that she had never experienced for a child before. She suddenly longed to be able to look after him until he could care for himself.

When Dr Eckhart returned a few minutes later, he found them still on the floor of the X-ray room. His surprise changed quickly to concern.

'What happened?' he asked.

'He had a *grand mal,*' Fiona replied softly, still crad-ling the little boy to her. 'He was so brave.'

The doctor knelt down beside her and took the child from her. He carried him back through to the consulting room and laid him once more upon the examination bed. Edmund was breathing quietly, his colour had returned and he looked like any other sleeping child.

'We'll have a look at the pictures, then take him home,' said his father.

The plates ruled out any fracture.

'Must be torn ligaments for that amount of oedema. He must have fallen hard.' Dr Eckhart scrutinised the X-rays with care, then turned to Fiona again. 'I'll as-pirate some of the abnormal synovial fluid and we'll put a compression dressing on and apply some ice packs. After twenty-four hours or so, some heat, and that should do the trick.'

Fiona began setting up a trolley with instruments for the aspiration, fetching a compression dressing and a dish of ice from one of the fridges. As she did so, she told her employer about Edmund's description of how his head had felt just before his fit.

'Has he ever had a fit before?' she asked anxiously. 'Will he be all right?'

Dr Eckhart looked up quickly from what he was doing, sensing more than purely professional concern in Fiona's voice. For a moment, she thought that he was angry. But when he spoke again his voice was gentle.

'No, he's never had one before,' he said. 'It must have been the bang on the head. These things happen some-times with children. I am not too worried about it, yet. Fiona, you are over-anxious. Yesterday and today . . .' He seemed to think better of what he was about to say. 'In a way it's good. He's fast asleep and can't feel any of this.' He gestured towards the aspiration cannula.

Fiona supported the child's leg while Dr Eckhart

applied the compression dressing. But she could not help worrying about Edmund's fit. Her head was full of fear of the worst.

As if he read her mind, the doctor threw her a hard look.

'It isn't a good idea to get too carried away with emotional involvement.'

Fiona felt suddenly ashamed. The little boy whose leg she now gently covered with a blanket again was this man's son. How could she be so selfishly forgetful of what he must be suffering?

'I'm sorry. Is there anything else I can do?' she stammered, acutely aware of his eyes on her face.

'If you really wish to help me further,' he said slowly, 'you might come back to my home with us. Edmund must be watched for the next twenty-four hours, and it would be extremely helpful if you could observe him.'

Fiona's heart turned over. She had dreaded parting from the child, yet thought her role fulfilled.

'There is nothing I would rather do than that,' she stated with quiet sincerity.

Hans Eckhart regarded her steadily.

'I shall bring the car round so that we don't have to take him too far through the snow,' he said, 'and if you collect your coat meanwhile, I'll be back for you both in a moment.'

CHAPTER TEN

IT WAS strange for Fiona to walk into the house which had been for so long part of her imaginings, but no spells were broken. The interior of the large chalet was more characterful and charming then even she had dreamed, and she was enchanted.

She followed Dr Eckhart up the wide wooden staircase to the first floor, where bedrooms opened off either side of a broad corridor. As he was carried through into his own bedroom, Edmund looked over his father's shoulder at Fiona—a sleepy glance of childish pride at the introduction of a new grown-up into his home.

The room Fiona found herself in was grand for a child's room; large and wood-panelled, with french windows leading out on to a broad balcony at the front of the house.

Dr Eckhart swiftly and gently undressed his small son, talking to him all the time although the child was still half asleep. Fiona stood back and was amazed at the tenderness with which Edmund was tucked into bed beneath his quilt, a teddy bear comfortably in beside him.

The doctor turned to Fiona at last, with some surprise, as if he had forgotten her presence in the room and was now embarrassed at her having witnessed the scene which had just taken place.

'You should try to get some sleep,' he said gruffly.

He moved some cushions and soft toys from a divan which stood along one wall. 'You must be tired. I do appreciate this extension of your normal duties. I hope it will not be necessary for you to continue observations all through the night, but you are the best judge of that. I shall make sure that you recoup these extra hours . . .'

Fiona recalled her long-ago reversed decision to take time off to go to England. Nothing was now further from her thoughts or wishes.

'It's no trouble,' she said quickly. 'I'm really pleased to be here; to be able to help.'

'Well,' he replied briskly, 'Helga will bring you something to eat in the morning, I am sure, and I will be in as soon as I can to see Edmund. I am on call over weekends, as you have probably guessed, and so if I am delayed it will be because I have been called out to a patient. But the little boy understands that.' He looked about him, gave Fiona a nod and then bade her goodnight.

'Goodnight, Dr Eckhart,' she responded.

After he had gone, she walked over to the french windows as the evening deepened into night. She had been touched by Dr Eckhart as he had revealed himself to her today. He worked so hard, almost as if his work was his life. Yet he seemed so devoted to his children and, Fiona admitted to herself with a stab of anguish, to that woman.

Fiona glanced over at the sleeping child on the other side of the room, dismissing the mist which had crept over her vision, telling herself that she must try to sleep for a few hours tonight. Edmund stirred, sighed and was still again.

She decided to record his pulse, blood pressure and respirations every two hours overnight, and to check his pupils at the same time. She was not sorry to miss even the slightest sign that his fit had been more than an isolated response to his fall.

Long years on call for theatre and frequent stints on nights working the irregular hours that emergency surgery demanded had given Fiona the ability to benefit from catnaps. In fact, she thought, she felt fresher as dawn arrived the next morning than she often had lately after a sleepless night in her own bed. She had not used the divan but had slept in an armchair between the two-hourly observations.

All night they had stayed steady. To her immeasurable relief there had been no sinister slowing of the pulse or respirations and no creeping rise in temperature. The dark pupils had reacted promptly and evenly to her torchlight. In fact, Edmund showed no sign of neurological disturbance.

'My knee hurts!'

Fiona smiled gently and helped the child to lift himself up into a sitting position. She plumped his pillows and arranged them so that they supported him.

'We'll have a look at it in a moment, when your father comes,' she said. 'How did you sleep?'

He had not moved as she measured his vital functions.

'I don't know,' he grinned, 'I was asleep.'

Fiona laughed. 'All right, clever boots,' she said.

'Why are you in my house?' he asked.

She was explaining when his father appeared, his eyes still sleepy. It was strange and exciting to see him here, at home. She became aware that she was staring at him and looked quickly away. But he had caught her eyes upon him.

Dr Eckhart picked up the chart which Fiona had been using to record the measurements she had taken, and read every mark and word she'd put upon it. His features were calm when at last he looked up again.

'So you're doing all right, little boy,' he announced affectionately. He sat down on the edge of Edmund's bed and tousled his hair. 'How does that knee feel?'

'It hurts,' repeated Edmund, without conviction.

While he examined the knee, the doctor explained the heat treatment that he was going to use to reduce the swelling. He also explained why it would work, and his son listened with fascination. Their relationship seemed so strong and loving. Fiona was struck by how close they were. It was almost as if they shared responsibility for the family; as if they felt they had to look after the women between them.

Dr Eckhart was covering up the now much less swollen knee and Fiona had barely formulated her thoughts when the two sisters tumbled into the sick-room, closely followed by the enormous Carl.

'Papa says you're very stupid and Carl is very clever,' said one of the girls, and Edmund looked up at his father questioningly.

'I said no such thing, mischief-maker,' he smiled. 'I said that Edmund could be foolish sometimes and that Carl was a hero.'

The two girls looked from their father to Fiona and back again, evidently trying to digest this remark.

Fiona glanced at Edmund, who stuck his tongue out swiftly at his sisters and giggled. The doctor exchanged a rather old-fashioned look with Fiona. Children had a magical way of stripping occasions and relationships of all formality.

'Why are you here, Sister?' the blonder of the two little girls wanted to know. 'Do you still go for long walks alone?'

'Sometimes,' Fiona smiled. 'But now I'm here to look after Edmund.'

'See?' said Edmund, as if he'd just won a prize.

'Anyway, we don't care,' said the other, older girl, making it plain that Edmund was indeed in an envied position. 'We're going to Interlaken with Helga.'

'Oh, Papa, can I go too?'

Edmund was crestfallen. He had forgotten this treat which had been promised the children for today.

Fiona watched the father shake his head solemnly.

'Sorry, no question of walking around on that leg

today. But I tell you what, I won't go into the clinic to do my boring old accounts today as usual on a Sunday. I'll stay here and play with you.'

'And *we*'re going to Interlaken,' crowed the girls in unison.

Edmund pouted and then looked as if he was going to cry.

'I want Fiona to stay with me,' he stated softly.

Dr Eckhart looked straight at Fiona, who was standing a little apart from the family group, watching snow fall over the far mountains. The day was white again. Not a day for spending outside.

'I was going to tell Sister that she could go home now,' the doctor told the children. 'She must be very tired. She has been looking after Edmund all the time we've been asleep, haven't you, Sister?'

'Please stay with me, Fiona.'

Edmund looked at her with grey-flecked eyes.

'Of course I will,' she said. 'We shall have a lovely day and you can show me all your toys.'

'Oh, can we stay too?' chorused the girls.

Fiona and her employer looked at one another and smiled.

'Certainly not!' he said. 'Fair's fair, isn't it, Edmund?'

He showed the two sisters and the dog to the door. 'Time to get your finery on if you're going to see Helga's smart friends. Come on. And I'll see you around lunchtime, young man. Don't tire Fiona out too greatly.'

He glanced at her and then he was gone, among the waving children who were already chattering about the day ahead. Fiona helped Edmund up and into the armchair and then remade his bed. She was just helping him back in when Helga appeared with two breakfasts upon an enormous tray.

The blonde placed the tray silently down upon a small table next to Edmund's bed. There were fresh rolls, jam, cheese and a selection of cold smoked meats as well as eggs and coffee for Fiona, fruit juice for Edmund.

Fiona thanked her warmly, and got a muttered, '*Bitte*', in response, the minimum courtesy that was possible. Although it was still early in the morning, the woman was immaculate. Younger than she had seemed from a distance away, she was made up and her silken hair was gathered gently into a ribbon at the nape of her neck. She wore a cream silk shirt and cord trousers that matched and looked elegant in her expensively casual outfit. Her brilliant blue eyes glanced antagonistically at Fiona and then rested more kindly upon Edmund.

'Fiona's staying with me today,' said the child proudly.

'Ah, so?'

Even Edmund seemed to sense that this topic of conversation was not worth pursuing. He shrugged and looked to Fiona for something to say. But the blonde was gone, closing the door softly behind her.

'She's funny sometimes, Helga,' said Edmund, munching a piece of bread.

Fiona sipped her hot coffee. She had no doubt now that the blonde deeply resented her presence in the house. There had been nothing funny about the way she'd been scrutinised. The woman disliked Fiona and had done from the first moment that their eyes had met, all those weeks ago. But why?

My mummy's dead—the child's words echoed in Fiona's head. Helga might not be married to Hans Eckhart, but she certainly felt that she was the woman of the household. Fiona forced herself to remember the gentle way Hans had handled Helga when she had fainted in the clinic.

Yet now it did not seem so odd that he had been so tender with her. Since then she had seen so much in him that she had never guessed was in his temperament.

There was a softness in his character. Perhaps he responded in that way instinctively when a woman was hurt. But then her mind flew back to his angry accusations and insinuations; to the bitter tears she'd shed.

The truth was that she no longer knew how to think or feel about the man at all. The picture that she had of him was changing too fast, too profoundly. She buttered a piece of bread and put jam on it unthinkingly. She needed sleep, she thought, and then she'd know how she felt.

But before then there was a whole morning to fill with games. Edmund taught her how to play Lotto and then told her some stories which he said he'd made up. Then they played Snakes and Ladders and then Scrabble, in German, which tested Fiona's still far from perfect usage too hard, so that he won game after game. This, of course, delighted him.

'You're fun!' he told her, after he had beaten her for the third successive time. 'Helga always beats me. She's a teacher, you know. The girls go to school during the week, but I'm too young and so Helga teaches me. She cooks nice dinners too.'

So! The doctor had found a bargain in the blonde, Fiona mused. Youth, brains, domestic capability and beauty too. What more could he possibly want? A nurse! She smiled wryly to herself. The only thing that this perfect creature appeared lacking in was the ability to nurse the family, a loophole neatly filled by herself. It was no use trying to pretend that the realisation did not hurt.

Around midday she went downstairs and, according to her small patient's instructions, found some lunch for them both. She had confidently expected Dr Eckhart to have returned by now, but she could not leave lunch any longer. Both she and Edmund were hungry from their morning at play.

The kitchen was at the back of the house. It had large windows from which Fiona knew she should be able to see up into the pine forests. But today she could see nothing but snowy whiteness. Everything in the kitchen was modern; two sinks in a long expanse of stainless steel draining-board, a black hob oven with a matching separate set of gas rings and matching fridge, dishwasher and washing-machine. The red-tiled floor was spotless, and so were the shining working surfaces, dotted with pretty dishes of fruit and vegetables.

Fiona loved the contrast between old and new that characterised the house, the old wood-panelled bedroom and this space-age kitchen. Everything seemed to have been chosen with such care. She found cold meat and salad in the fridge and arranged it, with glasses of milk, on a tray to take upstairs.

Edmund was recovering by the moment. After lunch, Fiona would take his pulse, blood pressure and temperature again, and then that would be that. Her official work would be finished. The boy's father would see to his knee when he got back, and she would go home to her flat—to bed.

'Papa will be back soon,' Edmund remarked, as if he read her thoughts, 'but Sundays are always so boring. You will stay, Fiona, won't you? Even after Papa comes home. Please?'

She smiled into the pleading eyes. She could lose her heart to this child—if she had not done so already. They began yet another game of Scrabble after lunch and it was much, much later that the telephone rang somewhere in the big house. Fiona ran to the door.

Out in the corridor, she could hear the tones clearly coming from a room two doors down from Edmund's.

'Yes? Fiona Shore here,' she said breathlessly when she found the phone.

'Fiona? It's me, Hans. I'm still at the clinic and I won't

be back for some time. I've got to go out. How is
Edmund?'

'Fine. We've been playing ever since you left. And
we've had some lunch. His observations are fine. I've
discontinued them now, as we agreed.'

'Good. Could you put some local heat to that knee? A
well-covered hot water bottle will do. I think you'll find
one in the bathroom next to the room you're in—if that's
my bedroom?'

For the first time since she'd lifted the phone, Fiona
looked about her and realised that she was indeed in a
large bedroom, and that she was in fact sitting on the
bed.

'I've got to go to Interlaken,' Hans continued, his
voice sounding slightly strained. 'Helga and the girls
went out in a borrowed car . . . I'll be back as soon as I
can. Fiona?'

'Yes, I'm listening. Don't worry about anything. I can
easily cope here. I shall take good care of Edmund.'

'Thank you, Fiona. You . . . I'll be back as soon as I
possibly can.'

'Okay,' she said. And then she heard the receiver click
down at his end. She hadn't told him what she had
wanted to tell him—to take care of himself. What if . . .?
Fiona looked out at the dangerous snow-filled land-
scape. She could see practically nothing. She must not
let Edmund see her fear.

Around her the room seemed to want to comfort her.
It was a sunny, lovely corner of the house with buttercup
and daisy colours everywhere and an exquisite hand-
made patchwork quilt on the bed.

'Your papa's been delayed,' she said as she returned
to the boy's bedroom, 'and so it looks as though we'll
have to entertain one another for the rest of the day after
all.'

'Hooray!' said Edmund.

'I'm going to put a warm hot water bottle next to your knee to help it get better, as your papa told you that it would, and then we'll find another game to play. But no more Scrabble!' she laughed. 'You're getting too good for me.'

'Do you think you could read to me, then?' Edmund asked seriously. 'Nobody ever seems to have time to read to me these days.'

'Of course. What shall we have?'

Fiona wandered over to a red bookcase which stood near the divan.

'There's *Winnie-the-Pooh* in English,' suggested the little boy shyly. 'My mummy was English, you know.'

'No,' said Fiona softly, 'I didn't know that, Edmund.'

She took the book down and gave it to him to look at the pictures while she went to fill his hot water bottle. So that explained little Edmund's perfect English, and his father's fluency too. Even very tiny children picked up two languages if they were both spoken at home.

She put the bottle in his bed and then went to pull the brightly coloured curtains at the windows. It was the time of day when afternoon and evening meet, and today the sky seemed to be married to the land. Everything was silver-white.

She read for a long time and then went downstairs to prepare soup and heat the end of a casserole that she found in the fridge. Again, she carried the meal upstairs to Edmund's room. At this, their third meal together, the atmosphere between them was warm and confiding.

'I love my papa,' announced Edmund as he finished his soup, 'and I love you too. I think you should marry him and come and live with us.'

'Oh, you do, do you?' Fiona grinned at her small charge.

'Yes,' said Edmund. 'Can you read me some more about Winnie-the-Pooh before I go to sleep?'

'Now that I *can* do,' smiled Fiona cryptically.

She read to him until his eyes no longer opened each time she paused for breath, and his breathing carried the quiet, sure rhythm of dreamless sleep.

The silence of the great house around her made Fiona feel ill at ease. She had not really been invited to stay here, and yet here she was in her employer's home with only the sleeping child upstairs to remind her of her reason for being here. Downstairs, she switched on the lights in the big hall to keep her company, and then did the same in the living-room.

How luxurious everything was! She wandered around looking at the water-colours that hung in the dining area and at the circular dining table with its big central arrangement of white lilies. Everywhere she sensed a woman's touch. But the touch of a perfectionist, lacking warmth and love. The more she thought like this, the sadder she felt.

Time was passing so slowly. Where was Hans? What had happened to the children? She sat down on one of the white chairs and then stood again, as if she did not belong in the room. She was restless and her imagination filled the empty minutes only too readily.

Two or three times the memory of what Edmund had told her of his mother returned—her nationality and how she died. The thought that Helga and the children might have come to harm appalled her. Such tragedy could not occur twice in a family. She pushed the thought aside.

Helga was such an unknown quantity; even Edmund referred oddly to her, as if she were neither mother nor sister to him. And Hans treated her strangely too. Fiona could not put her finger on what their relationship might be.

Once or twice she ran upstairs to check on Edmund,

but each time she discovered him sleeping peacefully, exactly as she had left him, his arm around his bear. Looking at his quiet face, Fiona cursed the feelings that he aroused in her; the sort of mother-love that she had never known in herself before. It did not seem to matter that she knew how inappropriate the moment was for them.

Coming back down into the hall for the second time, she noticed the telephone. The instrument that she had answered had been, as she had suspected, an extension. The main one stood on a high table in a slight recess in the hall, beneath the staircase. Looking down at it, she saw her name upon a notepad beside the phone.

Helga, the message read, *phone Sister Shore at the clinic and tell her I had to leave early. Tried to call her at home around six, but line engaged. Thanks, Hans.*

It was dated a week ago, the day that he had left for Geneva. Fiona realised that his call must have been blocked by Daniel's. Daniel, with his stupid determination to come to Wengen to get her back. And all her misery had been unfounded. Hans had not forgotten her at all.

But she had never got his message. Helga had not given her a call at the clinic. Instead she had smiled when she had shown Daniel to Fiona's place of work, confident that his presence in Wengen would occupy Fiona and deflect her from any personal interest in her employer. Fiona could see it all so clearly now. But she still could not understand the reason for the blonde's petty jealousy. She had not deserved it.

Fiona was still turning the thing over in her mind when she heard the front door open. She rushed into the hall to meet the white-faced subject of her puzzling who, with a child on each hand, pushed past Fiona and into the living-room. Hans Eckhart followed them in, but he did not ignore Fiona's presence. Instead, he put an arm around her gently and led her into the big room too. Then he sat her down in one of the white chairs before turning his attention to the children.

He took each of the girls coats and boots off in turn, then smoothed the hair back out of their tired faces. Then he went into the kitchen, returning shortly with mugs of steaming milk for the children and Helga, who lay back in a chair apparently utterly exhausted by her experience. The two little girls kept staring from Fiona to their father, while they sipped their drinks and the colour returned to their cheeks.

'Enough adventure for one day,' said Hans Eckhart.

Two, Fiona mentally corrected him.

Within half an hour of the front door opening, all three adventurers were upstairs in bed. Fiona remained where the doctor had sat her down, too numb with events, too tired to make sense of anything any more.

When he reappeared, Dr Eckhart went straight to the sideboard and poured two large balloon glasses of cognac.

'I need this,' he said, handing her one of the glasses of fiery liquid, 'and you certainly deserve it.'

Fiona was too amazed to speak. Instead she took a gulp of brandy and felt it course down her throat leaving a trail of molten gold behind it.

'That child!' Dr Eckhart was saying. 'She took the car from her friends so that she could drive to the station and then back if she missed the train to Lauterbrunnen. Terrified that she'd be late back and you and I might get an opportunity to develop our non-professional relationship . . .'

There was gentle humour in his eyes, but Fiona saw the strain of his last few hours there too. She heard what he said with sadness, but not surprise.

'But why?'

'Helga is young and she loves me like a father. She was

an orphan and came to work with us when she was just a child, only fifteen, as our au pair. The children were all babies then. She became almost one of the family, and the girls, particularly, indentified with her after my wife's death. Of course, she is so . . . feminine.'

Fiona listened motionless, unable even to lift her glass to her lips while her employer spoke quietly to her.

'Perhaps she developed some sort of schoolgirl crush on me, or perhaps she is simply nervous for me. She witnessed many unfortunate scenes while my wife was alive. And she knew what happened at the end . . . Anyway, she is over-protective in her child-like way, wanting me to be cared for and not hurt!'

He shrugged and smiled, as much as to indicate how ridiculous was the preoccupation of his au pair girl; as if he was not vulnerable. He smiled in self-deprecation. But Fiona had begun to understand by now that he was not made of granite.

'I'm afraid she has been very naughty about you, Fiona. She was anxious to tell me that you had a keen fiancé who had followed you here from England. She wanted me to be sure that you were not the woman I thought you were . . . and sometimes she almost convinced me. If she were not so marvellous with the girls . . . But we can talk about Helga later, about whether she stays or goes. She gave herself a bad scare, skidded . . .'

Fiona took another sip of brandy. She felt truly in need of it now.

'But thank goodness she is safe—and the girls,' she whispered.

The doctor paused. He gazed into his almost empty glass, then went over to the sideboard to replenish it. His back was still turned to her when next he spoke.

'Yes,' he said. 'My wife died on that stretch of road in conditions just such as today's.'

'Hans!' Fiona did not know what gave her the courage to go to him at that moment, but she did go to him. She took hold of his hand impulsively, as she had so often grasped that of a frightened patient.

But Hans Eckhart was not a frightened patient. He took her in his arms suddenly and with conviction, and for a long time he held her to him, hard and close. They stood locked together, neither speaking nor moving. Fiona felt the tension of the day beginning to turn itself into tears and she held her breath against them.

'It's all right, Fiona,' Hans whispered, cradling her head against his chest. 'Everything is going to be all right.'

He kissed her infinitely gently and slowly, as if to reassure her of time itself.

'Did you love her very much?' Fiona asked at last. 'Has it been very terrible for you?'

Dr Eckhart shook his head slowly and regarded Fiona with calm eyes. She felt totally defenceless under his gaze, aware that tendrils of her hair had escaped from the auburn coil which she had pinned roughly in place hours ago, aware of her tired eyes and her crumpled white dress. She dreaded hearing how much this man had loved his wife, and yet she longed for him to talk to her, to share his grief with her.

'I thought I loved her . . . once,' he began slowly. 'But now . . . She killed my feeling for her. She was so different. She loved the bright lights and hated living here. She could not understand my refusal to follow a career in the city, and she . . . When she died she was with Erich Zimmerman.' His voice was so low that Fiona could hear her own heart.

'Oh, God,' she breathed.

She took his hand again and he looked away from her, as if recalling a far memory.

'He was driving,' he said without bitterness, as if the

pain was long-past. 'It was not the first time that they had been together, and he was not the first man. He walked away from the accident unharmed.'

The shock of his words reverberated through Fiona, but her eyes did not leave the flecked gaze of the man before her. In her mind she saw his gentle smile as he comforted Erich's mother and his skilful care when he examined the ski instructor.

'She was a beautiful creature, but not as beautiful as you, Fiona,' Hans Eckhart said. He lifted her face to him and his words seemed to hang in the air like butterflies, too fragile for her to touch. 'And she lacked your inner beauty too. Yet you reminded me so painfully of her at first that I could hardly bear to be in your company. She was the nurse of the clinic before you.'

A moment or two passed in which Fiona relived and made new sense of so much of the past weeks that she felt dizzy. When she had brought her attention back to Hans again he was smiling at her with sadness in his eyes.

'That time with Erich, when you saw us together, and then with Daniel,' Fiona began, 'you must understand . . .'

'It's all right, Fiona, I know. I have been very unfair to you. And you do not have to justify yourself to me.'

'But it was all so terribly wrong and ironical. That you must have thought . . . when the only man I was thinking about was you.' It was a relief to say it at last, no matter what happened now.

'Is that true, Fiona?'

'Yes,' she whispered.

He drew her towards him again and began to kiss her face; covering her eyes, her forehead with kisses; and then her lips. She returned his kisses, shyly at first, and then with all the depth of feeling that had grown unshown inside her for so long.

The big house around them, Helga, the sleeping

children, the Weiss Kreuz Klinik, the past and the future—all receded. Only the texture of his skin, his special touch, the warmth of him and the certainty of their kisses existed. Fiona awoke as from a dream.

'Do you like Wengen, Fiona?'

'Yes,' she murmured, 'I like it very much.' She could taste his kisses as she spoke and her body seemed merged with his, although now he was holding her quite lightly.

'I told you that I thought once that I loved my wife,' he began, 'and that was true. But now I know that the feeling that I had for her was not love or even respect. I thought you beautiful, Fiona, right from the first time I saw you on the train in Lauterbrunnen, and then I learned to respect you both professionally and personally. You were so brave in the face of my rage and anguish. Many times I felt sure that I must lose you, and I hated myself for lacking your courage. I would never have forgiven myself for not being brave enough to love you, Fiona. And I do love you.'

She put her hand on his chest over the place where she could feel his heart beating, and she felt her own life answering his.

'I love you too,' she said.

They held one another for a long time.

After a while he said, 'I should like to take you out for dinner.'

'Thank you,' she smiled, 'but I should like to change first.' She spread her arms in a gesture of mock disgust at her own appearance.

'That lovely black silk dress?'

'It's the only one I've got.'

'It will always be my favourite.'

Fiona smiled at Hans and then ran her hands through her loosened hair in momentary nervousness, as if none of this could be true.

'Fiona,' he said quietly, 'if I ask you a question, will you promise not to say no? Will you promise not to be too unromantic about a holiday in the Caribbean and not to say goodnight to me ever again outside in the snow?'

'Yes,' Fiona said, laughing. 'Yes, yes, yes.' And she kissed him three times to seal her promises.

Doctor Nurse Romances

Amongst the intense emotional pressures of modern medical life, doctors and nurses often find romance. Read about their lives and loves in the other two Doctor Nurse titles available this month.

HEART MURMURS
by Grace Read

After a childhood spent in Care, Sister Chloe Kingsley has a special sympathy for the underprivileged children on her ward. And it's that rare understanding which attracts the attention of paediatrician Dr Miles Bredon. But he is heir to a fortune — an important man — and Chloe knows that a girl from her background could never satisfy him...

CINDERELLA SRN
by Anna Ramsay

Transformed, like Cinderella, for a single night, Nurse Kate Cameron goes to Stambridge Royal's Christmas Ball and finds herself in the arms of a mysterious and attractive stranger. But a fairytale ending seems out of the question when, in real life, this Cinderella has chapped hands and an unflattering uniform and Prince Charming turns out to be Luke Harvey, the new senior registrar!

Mills & Boon
the rose of romance

Mills & Boon

4 Doctor Nurse Romances
FREE

Coping with the daily tragedies and ordeals of a busy hospital, and sharing the satisfaction of a difficult job well done, people find themselves unexpectedly drawn together. Mills & Boon Doctor Nurse Romances capture perfectly the excitement, the intrigue and the emotions of modern medicine, that so often lead to overwhelming and blissful love. By becoming a regular reader of Mills & Boon Doctor Nurse Romances you can enjoy SIX superb new titles every two months plus a whole range of special benefits: your very own personal membership card, a free newsletter packed with recipes, competitions, bargain book offers, plus big cash savings.

**AND an Introductory FREE GIFT for YOU.
Turn over the page for details.**

Fill in and send this coupon back today
and we'll send you
**4 Introductory
Doctor Nurse Romances yours to keep**
FREE.

At the same time we will reserve a
subscription to Mills & Boon
Doctor Nurse Romances for you. Every
two months you will receive the latest
6 new titles, delivered direct to your door.
You don't pay extra for delivery. Postage and
packing is always completely Free.
There is no obligation or commitment –
you receive books only for
as long as you want to.

It's easy! Fill in the coupon below and return it to
**MILLS & BOON READER SERVICE, FREEPOST, P.O. BOX 236,
CROYDON, SURREY CR9 9EL.**

Please note: **READERS IN SOUTH AFRICA write to
Mills & Boon Ltd., Postbag X3010,
Randburg 2125, S. Africa.**

- - - - - - - - - - - - - - - - - - -

FREE BOOKS CERTIFICATE

**To: Mills & Boon Reader Service, FREEPOST, P.O. Box 236,
Croydon, Surrey CR9 9EL.**

Please send me, free and without obligation, four Dr. Nurse Romances, and reserve a Reader
Service Subscription for me. If I decide to subscribe I shall receive, following my free parcel of
books, six new Dr. Nurse Romances every two months for £6.00*, post and packing free. If I
decide not to subscribe, I shall write to you within 10 days. The free books are mine to keep in
any case. I understand that I may cancel my subscription at any time simply by writing to you. I
am over 18 years of age.
Please write in BLOCK CAPITALS.

Name _____

Address _____

_____

_____ Postcode _____

SEND NO MONEY — TAKE NO RISKS

EP15